# RUN FOR YOUR LIFE

## M A COMLEY

JEAMEL PUBLISHING LIMITED

New York Times and USA Today bestselling author M A Comley
Published by Jeamel Publishing limited
Copyright © 2020 M A Comley
Digital Edition, License Notes

All rights reserved. This book or any portion thereof may not be reproduced, stored in a retrieval system, transmitted in any form or by any means electronic or mechanical, including photocopying, or used in any manner whatsoever without the express written permission of the author, except for the use of brief quotations in a book review or scholarly journal.

This is a work of fiction. Names, characters, places and incidents are a product of the author's imagination or are used fictitiously, and any resemblance to actual persons living or dead, business establishments, events or locales is entirely coincidental.

Irrational Justice (a 10,000 word short story)

Seeking Justice (a 15,000 word novella)

Caring For Justice (a 24,000 word novella)

Savage Justice (a 17,000 word novella Featuring THE UNICORN)

Vile Justice (A 17,000 word novella)

Clever Deception (co-written by Linda S Prather)

Tragic Deception (co-written by Linda S Prather)

Sinful Deception (co-written by Linda S Prather)

Forever Watching You (DI Miranda Carr thriller)

Wrong Place (DI Sally Parker thriller #1)

No Hiding Place (DI Sally Parker thriller #2)

Cold Case (DI Sally Parker thriller#3)

Deadly Encounter (DI Sally Parker thriller #4)

Lost Innocence (DI Sally Parker thriller #5)

Goodbye, My Precious Child (DI Sally Parker #6)

Web of Deceit (DI Sally Parker Novella with Tara Lyons)

The Missing Children (DI Kayli Bright #1)

Killer On The Run (DI Kayli Bright #2)

Hidden Agenda (DI Kayli Bright #3)

Murderous Betrayal (Kayli Bright #4)

Dying Breath (Kayli Bright #5)

Taken (Kayli Bright #6 coming March 2020)

The Hostage Takers (DI Kayli Bright Novella)

No Right to Kill (DI Sara Ramsey #1)

Killer Blow (DI Sara Ramsey #2)

The Dead Can't Speak (DI Sara Ramsey #3)

Deluded (DI Sara Ramsey #4)

The Murder Pact (DI Sara Ramsey #5)

# ALSO BY M A COMLEY

Blind Justice (Novella)

Cruel Justice (Book #1)

Mortal Justice (Novella)

Impeding Justice (Book #2)

Final Justice (Book #3)

Foul Justice (Book #4)

Guaranteed Justice (Book #5)

Ultimate Justice (Book #6)

Virtual Justice (Book #7)

Hostile Justice (Book #8)

Tortured Justice (Book #9)

Rough Justice (Book #10)

Dubious Justice (Book #11)

Calculated Justice (Book #12)

Twisted Justice (Book #13)

Justice at Christmas (Short Story)

Justice at Christmas 2 (novella)

Prime Justice (Book #14)

Heroic Justice (Book #15)

Shameful Justice (Book #16)

Immoral Justice (Book #17)

Toxic Justice (Book #18)

Overdue Justice (Book #19)

Unfair Justice (a 10,000 word short story)

Twisted Revenge (DI Sara Ramsey #6)

The Lies She Told (DI Sara Ramsey #7)

For The Love Of… (DI Sara Ramsey #8)

Run For Your Life (DI Sara Ramsey #9) Coming August 2020

I Know The Truth (A psychological thriller )

The Caller (co-written with Tara Lyons)

Evil In Disguise – a novel based on True events

Deadly Act (Hero series novella)

Torn Apart (Hero series #1)

End Result (Hero series #2)

In Plain Sight (Hero Series #3)

Double Jeopardy (Hero Series #4)

Criminal Actions (Hero Series #5)

Regrets Mean Nothing (Hero #6)

Sole Intention (Intention series #1)

Grave Intention (Intention series #2)

Devious Intention (Intention #3)

Merry Widow (A Lorne Simpkins short story)

It's A Dog's Life (A Lorne Simpkins short story)

A Time To Heal (A Sweet Romance)

A Time For Change (A Sweet Romance)

High Spirits

The Temptation series (Romantic Suspense/New Adult Novellas)

Past Temptation

Lost Temptation

Cozy Mystery Series

Murder at the Wedding

Murder at the Hotel

Murder by the Sea

Tempting Christa (A billionaire romantic suspense co-authored by Tracie Delaney #1)

Avenging Christa (A billionaire romantic suspense co-authored by Tracie Delaney #2)

# ACKNOWLEDGMENTS

Thank you as always to my rock, Jean, I'd be lost without you in my life.

Special thanks as always go to @studioenp for their superb cover design expertise.

My heartfelt thanks go to my wonderful editor Emmy Ellis, my proofreaders Joseph, Barbara and Jacqueline for spotting all the lingering nits.

Thank you also to Barbara and Maria from my amazing ARC group who allowed me to use their names in this book.

To Mary, gone, but never forgotten. I hope you found the peace you were searching for my dear friend.

# PROLOGUE

*His* is chest rose and fell as he lay in wait…

Here came his target, drunk as a bloody lord.

*It should make the task easier than predicted.*

Hunter followed Douglas Connor from the pub, ensuring the shadows along the route disguised his progress. Jubilation seeped into his veins the second Connor turned into the park, close to his home. He'd watched this guy for weeks; most of the time he took this route home. It had been a gamble that had paid off. His vehicle was parked on the other side, in anticipation.

Connor staggered through the park, singing, if that's what you could call it, his own rendition of *You'll Never Walk Alone,* chuckling as he stumbled over the grass verge he was trying to stick to along the tarmac path. Now and then he peered over his shoulder, as if he knew someone was following him.

When Hunter sensed Connor was about to turn around, he hid behind a nearby tree. The exit was a few hundred yards ahead of them. Conscious of that, Hunter upped his pace, doing his best to stick to the grass, deadening the sound of his footsteps. His adrenaline had kicked up a notch and was the driving force to his actions now. His breathing came in short, sharp bursts the closer he got to what was to become his first victim. All that lay ahead of him was to become a learning curve, he knew and appreciated that much.

He was out of his comfort zone for sure, but his desire would overcome that. Connor had to be punished for the scandalous act he'd committed. He and the others, they would all receive their punishment, one by one.

It was time to make his move. Connor looked behind him again. This time, he was right there, in his face, a masked assailant, dressed all in black so he melded into his surroundings easily.

"What the…? Who are you?" Connor slurred, his head as wobbly as the legs trying to hold him upright.

"You'll find out soon enough. You and me are going to take a ride."

"What? I ain't goin' nowhere with you, man. Not in this lifetime or the next."

"We'll see about that." Hunter removed the squat metal bar from up his sleeve and clobbered Connor on the head.

The great oaf instantly dropped to the ground. Shit! He hadn't expected that. Now all he had to do was lift the chunky bastard.

Hunter yanked Connor to his feet and tipped him over his shoulder.

*Shit! He's heavier than I thought. What if someone sees me dragging the fucker to the van? What the heck was I thinking? It's too late to worry about that now. Too late to back out. My plan has been brewing for months. I need to get this first one over and done with. Everything will slot into place better then, once the first one is out of the way. Fat bastard. Ever heard of Slimming World, mate? It works wonders, for most people anyway.*

The exit was within spitting distance ahead. A noise alerted him, forcing him backwards behind a thick tree trunk. A young couple, laughing and chatting, walked past. He closed his eyes, praying Connor didn't stir and give them away. His heartbeat thundering in his ears, he waited another few seconds and then left his hiding place.

A strength he never knew existed emerged from somewhere, aiding him in his endeavours to get his prey to the vehicle. Suddenly, he regretted parking the van right next to a streetlight. It was amateurish. He should have put more thought into that part of the plan. He made a note to do better in the future because there was definitely a *next time* on the cards.

After lugging Connor's heavy frame into the back of the van, he whacked him over the head a second time and injected him with a sedative to ensure he didn't wake up during the twenty-minute journey, then he jumped in the driver's seat and took off, not an ounce of remorse in his veins. Instead, his mind whirred with the idea of what he had in store for his captive. His thoughts elsewhere, he neglected to see the lorry heading straight towards him until the last minute.

"What the fuck is wrong with you, moron? Learn to fucking drive properly. Foreign shits driving on the wrong side of the road, he could have killed me."

At that thought he laughed, imagining the police showing up to find him sitting in the front and an unconscious fat guy lying in the back. *That would have confused them, wouldn't it?*

Twenty minutes later, he drove down the wooded dirt track to the cabin and hauled his captive's body roughly out of the back, not giving a shit about whether this guy was hurting or not as he bounced onto the ground. This was just the beginning, there were many more painful moments ahead of Connor.

He tied Connor's hands with rope and placed him on the old, stained couch which he'd rescued from the tip on one of his many trips to furnish this place. It wasn't his permanent home, not by a long shot, so he didn't see the fun in throwing good money at it to decorate it properly. This was a getaway cabin for him, for when things got too much and he felt the world closing in on him. He would come here, to chill out for a few days, to put everything back into perspective. It usually worked—well, most of the time. Now, though, now he'd decided this place would have a different use entirely over the coming weeks.

With Connor safely secured, he filled the kettle from the bottle of water he'd fetched from the car and made himself a cup of coffee. He glanced around the room. There was a wooden-framed single bed in the corner with its numerous blankets to keep out the chill, even at this time of year. In the other corner was the door to the small shower room, something he'd constructed himself once he'd purchased the place from a friend of his a few years back.

No one knew about this place, only his friend, and there was no way Trevor could tell anyone about his secret den, not now he was living on the other side of the world in New Zealand.

Hunter sat there, mug of coffee in his hands, staring at Connor. The man repulsed him, and the thought of what he'd done five years before, well, it filled him with rage and a justification for bringing him here and what was in Connor's immediate future. The bastard wouldn't like it, but shit happened. Annoyed that 'fatboy' was still zonked out, he kicked him in the leg. "Wake up, you, useless prick."

Nothing. No movement at all. *Did I go too far, whacking him a second time on the head?* Nah, he doubted it. He crossed the cabin and picked up the water bottle, aimed it at Connor's face and squeezed it. The water gushed out, dousing his captive who spluttered awake. "Ah, nice of you to join me at last."

"Who are you? What do you want from me? What...why are my hands tied?"

"Questions, questions. The 'who' part can wait, you don't need to know that yet. The 'what' part, well, in response to that, nothing. And the 'why', that's a dumb question that really doesn't warrant an answer, not yet. Have you managed to sleep off your boozy state?"

Connor shook his head and cringed. "No. My head still hurts."

He laughed. "That's more likely down to the wallops I gave you."

"Why? What have I ever done to you?" Connor whined.

Hunter's gaze narrowed as the real reason why they were there rattled through his mind. No, he wouldn't visit that, not yet. "Believe me, I have a good reason to be holding you. Now shut up. The more you talk, the more incensed you're gonna make me. You really don't want that, I can assure you."

"Okay. Can I get a drink? My mouth is as dry as a sandpit."

"I just gave you water. Be grateful for small mercies." Hunter laughed.

"What? I need water."

Hunter tilted his head and sneered, "You really think you're in a position to make any demands?"

Connor swallowed. It echoed around the confined space. "I wasn't making any demands, all I was doing was asking for a drink, which I'm entitled to."

Hunter rushed at him and stuck his nose close to Connor's, barely two inches between them. "Are you arguing with me?"

Connor leaned back. "No. I'm sorry. I would never do that. Please, please forgive me."

"For what? Your past sins?"

"I haven't got any."

Hunter retreated a few steps. "Really? You might want to rethink that, and quickly, before my temper rises again."

"No. I don't need to. I've done nothing wrong."

"You really are an ignorant knobhead." His blood seared the veins beneath the surface of his skin. He bit down on the angry retort filling his mouth. The guy was only making matters worse, denying the wrong he'd committed. Never mind, tomorrow, at first light, he would get his comeuppance.

Instead of arguing the toss with Connor, he went in search of his holdall and removed his weapon of choice, a Winchester rifle. He'd practised long and hard over the past few months, enough to consider himself to be a crack shot. Connor would find out how much of an expert he'd become soon enough. He tinkered with his gear under the watchful gaze of his captive audience. His gaze connected with Connor's every few minutes as he prepared the other equipment in the holdall—a hunting knife, cartridges for the rifle and a set of binoculars. Adrenaline pumped around his system; he knew he wouldn't be able to sleep tonight, not with the excitement rushing through him.

"Please, what are you going to do with me?" Connor asked, his voice taut with nervousness.

"You'll see in the morning. Go to sleep. And yes, that's an order. You're gonna need your rest for what I have planned for you at first light, when no one else is around out here."

"I'm sorry if I've wronged you in the past. I have some money put away, maybe I can take out a loan, get you a few grand more, what do you say?"

He glared at him. "Money means fuck all to me, just so you know. Look at you, you're a snivelling no-good piece of shit. Not so big now, are you? You know, without your frigging mates egging you on, eh?"

Connor's eyes narrowed for a second or two as if he was contemplating what he'd said, and then his eyes extended, realisation hitting him with force. He mumbled something incoherent.

"Sorry, what was that, shithead?"

"Nothing. Oh God! I know what this is about. I'm so sorry—"

"La la la…I don't wanna hear it. After five years then being tied up here, now you think it's the right time to feel some form of remorse. It ain't gonna do you much good, not now. Get some sleep."

"You think I'm going to be able to do that, knowing what lies ahead of me?" Connor's gaze drifted to the equipment.

"Frankly, I don't give a fucking shit. I'm gonna get some kip. I suggest you do the same if you know what's good for you."

"Please, I didn't know what I was doing back then, none of us did. We were young and our hormones were raging…"

"What the fuck? You think that's a good enough excuse to justify what you frigging did? The damage you effing caused? Your mind must be so screwed up if that's what you believe. We've spoken enough, and frankly, you're boring the hell out of me. Get to sleep, you have a long day ahead of you tomorrow, we both have." He packed his equipment away and tucked the holdall under the single bed then slipped beneath the pile of blankets, not caring if Connor was cold or not. While he drifted off to sleep, Connor muttered to himself. At one point, he thought he gasped and caught a sob, or maybe that was wishful thinking on his part.

At five, the sun's rays warmed his face. He stretched the knots out of his back and shoulders and sat up. Connor was staring at him, his eyes bloodshot, and he looked bewildered.

"Morning. Sleep well, did we?"

"No, not at all, but I doubt if you care, right?"

"You've hit the nail on the head, arsehole, I don't give a flying fuck. Want some coffee?"

"Yes, please, milk and three sugars."

He slung his legs over the side of the bed and waved a finger at Connor. "Don't go thinking this is the Ritz and that you can place an order for breakfast, shithead. Coffee, black and no sugar is all that's on offer this morning, you hear me?"

"Okay, that's fine with me. I didn't mean to anger you."

"You haven't, no more than I was already, and stop trying to suck up to me, it won't work."

"I wasn't, I swear."

"Shut the fuck up. I hate people tweeting on at this time of the ruddy morning, got that?"

"Yes, I'm sorry. It won't happen again, I…"

Hunter shot him another warning glare, and Connor squeezed his lips together to prevent his tongue wagging.

While Hunter made the coffees, he whistled a merry tune. A tune that would remain with him during his morning exploits. He couldn't help wondering if Connor recognised what he was whistling. He chuckled. *Daddy's Gone a Hunting* had been a favourite of his growing up. Now he was living the dream, so to speak. He was eager to get on, no intention of having breakfast until the deed was over, so the coffee would have to suffice for now.

He placed the mug in front of Connor and stared down at him. "Enjoy."

"Umm…I don't want to bother you, but my hands are tied. How do you propose I drink it?"

Shrugging, Hunter turned away and sat on the edge of his bed. "Not my problem, pal."

Connor's mouth dropped open.

Hunter tilted his head. "Something you want to say?"

"No, sorry. I'm grateful for the smell, if nothing else, it's very refreshing."

"Good, you're not disappointed then, are you?" He sipped noisily at his coffee, all the while staring at his captive, thoughts of their upcoming adventure playing like a mini film clip through his mind. "Not long to go now," he murmured, a smile pulling his lips apart, baring his white teeth.

"Please, I don't know what your intentions are, but I'm begging you to reconsider. There must be some way out of this, there has to be."

"There isn't. Get used to the idea that you're not long for this earth, dickhead, but first, I'm going to have a little fun with you. Put the fear of God in you."

Connor's head dipped, his chin resting on his puffed-out chest. "I didn't mean it. I can't keep apologising. It was the biggest mistake of my life and—"

"I know, I know, you're going to take those regrets to your grave, right? Well, I'm glad to oblige in bringing your remorse out at last, it took long enough to bloody surface. What are you, twenty-four or twenty-five?"

"Twenty-four. You see, I've grown up since then. I knew it was a mistake, I tried to right that wrong but…"

"Don't give me that bullshit, you lying shit."

"I did. You have to believe me."

"Here's the thing: I don't have to believe a word you say. You're a worthless piece of scum, that's what you are. It's going to be a pleasure finishing you off. Now sup up. Oh, sorry, you can't. Okay, let's get this show on the road." He placed his empty mug in the small stone sink and crossed the room to stand in front of his captive.

Connor kicked out at him, earning another wallop to his head, this time from Hunter's clenched fist.

"Don't be a smartarse, it's not going to do you any good. Now, get up, fuckface."

He yanked him to his feet. At first, Connor resisted, swung around like a cat's toy on a piece of string—that was until Hunter kicked him in the leg.

"Get up. Don't mess with me, boy."

"I'm sorry. I'm scared. Please, won't you reconsider? Don't do this to me."

"Did you? Reconsider your disgusting actions back then? No. So don't have the frigging audacity to expect me to do it now. Your sort make me want to vomit. You think you're fucking it when you're going around in a gang, don't ya? Makes you feel all important, don't it? Well, where's all that courage and spunk gone now, eh?"

One final yank, and Connor was on his feet. "Please, please…," he stuttered, over and over.

"There's no need to beg, you'll get what's coming to you, sooner than you think. Are you ready now?"

"No. I'll never be ready."

He punched the whinging shit in his stomach, his fist disappearing into the folds of fat overhanging his belt.

"That hurt. Don't, please, no more."

"Okay, you've got your wish. Let's get on with it, we've wasted too much time as it is."

He retrieved his holdall and pushed Connor out of the front door. The sun seeped through the gaps in the trees and bathed them in its morning's warmth. Hunter raised his face, enjoying the sensation and willing the sun to give him the extra strength he needed to see this through.

His first kill…

# 1

Mark brought Sara her breakfast in bed. He was up early because he had an operation on a dog to perform first thing and needed to get his mini-theatre prepared before the dog arrived for its pre-op medication at eight-thirty. "Coffee and beans on toast with bacon, that should set you up for the day."

Sara scrambled to sit upright and puffed her pillows up behind her. Mark placed the tray on her lap and pecked her on the lips.

"Bloody hell, you didn't have to go to this much trouble."

"Are you seriously complaining?"

She grinned. "Only a little. I truly appreciate it, no, *you*, more than you'll ever know."

"I know you do. Let's make a pact never to take each other for granted, ever."

"Deal. Hey, where's all this coming from?"

He scratched his head and let out a small sigh. "Nothing. I'm conscious that you've been married before and you know what to expect from a husband. I hope I don't let you down."

"Whoa! Hang on a minute, buster. You could never do that. Is there something else troubling you?"

"Apart from a touch of wedding jitters possibly, no, nothing in the slightest."

"What are you saying? You want to call it off?"

He paced the floor beside the bed anxiously. "No, definitely not. Jesus, ignore me. I'm sorry, this isn't me trying to avoid the issue, I promise, but I have to shoot off."

"What about breakfast?"

"I'll grab something later." He kissed the top of her head and rushed out of the bedroom. The front door slammed shut a few seconds later.

*Wow! What was that all about?* Her appetite appeared to have gone with him. She picked at her breakfast, her mind constantly mulling over his words and what appeared to be his panicked expression. One thought in particular struck fear into her gut: was Mark getting cold feet?

She pushed the tray of uneaten breakfast to one side, along with her wayward thoughts, and hopped in the shower. It wouldn't hurt her to get into work early for a change. The alternative would be to sit in bed and dwell on what had just happened.

Downstairs in the kitchen, Misty wound herself around her legs while she washed up the breakfast pots and pans. "I knew there was a reason I don't succumb to eating a big breakfast during the week and only manage to grab a piece of toast most days. Bloody mess, look at it."

After she'd fed Misty, let her out of the back door and waited for her beloved cat to return, Sara secured the house and left for work. At least leaving home early would ensure she'd have a clear run into the city for a change, no chance of getting caught up in the usual dross of traffic.

The desk sergeant greeted her warmly. "Morning, ma'am. Another lovely day out there?"

"It is that, Jeff. Let's hope another case doesn't turn up to spoil it, eh?"

"Oh dear, I fear you've tempted fate there."

Sara sniggered and waited for Jeff to buzz her through the internal door. As expected, she was the first of her team to arrive. Sara crossed the room, picked up an obligatory coffee from the vending machine and immersed herself in paperwork for the next hour or so. Carla, her partner of three years, knocked on the door and joined her not long after she'd finished her onerous chore for the day.

"Hey, come in. How are things?"

Carla shrugged. "Same old. Did Mark kick you out of bed earlier than usual?"

"I'll have you know he brought me breakfast in bed this morning before he left to do an op."

"Bloody hell, I wish Gary would do that for me now and again. It always seems to be me being the one bending over backwards to care for him."

"And you do it so well, considering you work full time, love. All the wedding plans sorted out now?"

Carla waved the suggestion away. "No point me getting involved in that."

"Sorry? It's your big day, what are you talking about?"

"His mother has well and truly dug her heels in. We either do things her way or not at all."

"Wow, and you're allowing her to get her way about that?"

"I can't do anything about it. Every time I broach the subject, Gary throws a fit. His mum is footing the bill."

"Ah, I see. A case of my way or the highway, right?"

Carla tapped the side of her nose and nodded. "You've got it. I can't wait for it to be over and done with. Only a month to go. You've got two weeks left, yes?"

"Yep." Sara chewed the inside of her mouth.

"Why am I sensing some reluctance?"

"Not on my part. Mark, on the other hand, was acting a little weird this morning. Refused to elucidate on what was going on in his head, then he shot off. I suppose everything will turn out to be all right in the end."

"Have you got any doubts about that? You know, whether you're doing the right thing marrying him?"

"No. I've never been more sure about things." She tilted her head. "Are you?"

Carla's gaze drifted out of the window, and she sighed. "Sometimes I love him so much it hurts and, well, others, I can't stand to be near him."

"Since when? Bloody hell, girl, you can't marry him if you have huge doubts like that."

Carla turned to face her, tears dripping onto her cheeks. "I'm in too deep now to back out."

"Nonsense. Jesus, it would cause more damage if you said nothing, went through the ceremony, and the marriage failed after you've said your vows. Want to talk about it?"

"Not really. It's a blessed relief to come to work most days to get away from his foul moods and his mother constantly badgering me about this or that in regard to the wedding. I can understand why some folks think it's one of the most stressful times of their lives. Is it worth it? That's the question I find myself asking more often than not."

"Poor you. You know I'm always here for you if you ever need to vent."

"I know. I've tried not to rain on your parade, though. Everything is slotting into place perfectly with your own wedding. The last thing I want to do is spoil things for you."

"You could never do that. If you need to talk about things my door is always open, plus, I'm always there on the end of the phone when we're off duty, you know that."

"I know. I just feel daft talking about it, truth be told."

"Look, Carla, cards on the table. You should be jittery with nerves of excitement, not having massive reservations at this stage. Maybe take a few days off to reassess what you truly want out of life because entering a marriage with your heels firmly dug in the ground isn't the right thing to do at all."

"I hear you."

"What's Gary's view on things?"

"He hasn't really said much. He's concentrating on his rehabilitation, and the stress involved in that is excruciating at times. He's committed, I've never seen him so determined to get back to work full time."

"Maybe things will work out for the best when that becomes a reality. Can't you talk to him?"

"Nope, not really. Every time I raise the subject, he pooh-poohs it and says his mother has that side of things all in hand and to leave well alone. Between you and me…"

"Don't stop there. Get it off your chest, love."

"I dread the topic rearing its head. Go on, tell me that's not natural."

"It's not. You need to call a halt to things if that's how you truly feel, love." The phone on Sara's desk rang. She held up a finger. "Hold that thought." Then she answered it. "DI Ramsey. How can I help?"

"I need you over here ASAP."

"Lorraine?"

"Doh! Yes. I'm at a murder scene and I need your assistance."

"Where? And there's no need to take that tone with me."

"Sorry. At Elm Leigh Woods. Do you know it?"

"Hang on, I'll ask Carla. Do you know Elm Leigh Woods?"

Carla nodded and fished out her phone. "Yes. I'll get the satnav details for you."

"Okay, Carla knows it. We'll see you soon."

"A warning for you, it ain't pretty. Get suited and booted and hunt me out. We're deep into the woods. Follow the markers; we've put crime scene tape around the trees."

"Great. Just what I wanted to hear first thing. We'll see you soon." Sara ended the call and shot out of her chair.

Carla had already left the office and alerted the team.

"Hang tight until we get in touch, guys. Make sure all the paperwork on the previous cases is tied up while we're out." Sara hitched on her jacket and tapped her partner on the shoulder. "Are you ready to go?"

"Yep, just have to nip to the loo first."

"I'll be waiting in the car." Sara raced down the stairs and through the reception area.

"Well, someone's in a rush," Jeff yelled.

"A murder in the woods, Jeff."

"Oops…okay, best of luck with that one," he shouted after her before the outer door slammed shut.

Carla was a few minutes behind her. Sara used the siren to ease through the traffic in the city centre. If it was okay for the ambulances in Hereford to use them regularly then it was definitely okay for her to do the same.

The forest was a good twenty-minute drive from the station going in an easterly direction. They pulled up at the scene and spotted the SOCO van and Lorraine's vehicle at the entrance.

Sara pointed to the tape twined around a tree stump in the distance. "There. She told me to watch out for the trail she'd left. Let's get suited. We'll leave our protective shoes off for now."

They tore through the trees, and by the time they reached Lorraine and the rest of her team they were both out of breath. They slipped the covers over their shoes.

"Bloody hell. That was a trek and a half. How did the body get out here?"

"Good to see you, too." Lorraine smiled at her. "Spot-on question. My take is that the person was tracked through the woods and bumped off out here."

"Tracked? As in, you think they were hunted down?"

Lorraine nodded slowly, but it soon gained momentum. "My assumption in a nutshell. Over here, I'll show you why I think that."

The three of them approached the body lying amongst the sodden leaves beneath a huge oak tree. Its aim in the forest appeared to be to block out the sunlight, casting the area in an eerie atmosphere that sent chills scampering up Sara's spine.

"Are we all clear, guys?" Lorraine asked.

Two SOCO members gave her the thumbs-up and shifted their equipment back a few feet to allow them access to the body.

"Meet our John Doe," Lorraine announced, her arm sweeping over the corpse.

"I take it there's no ID then?"

"You assume right. Great start for you, I know."

"Yeah, not the best. Walk me through the rest of what we have here."

The corpse was lying on his front. Lorraine pointed out the bullet wounds in his back, neck and both legs. "I have no idea at this point which one caused his death. I'm guessing it was either the one to the back or the one to his neck."

"Shit! I hate the fact he was shot, here in Hereford. That's unheard of, isn't it?"

"Not unheard of but, I agree, it is rare for this area."

"Ugh…so, you think someone was chasing him through the woods and using him as some form of moving target?"

"Very good. Yep, that's my summation, given his injuries."

"Bloody hell. Let's hope this is a one-off and doesn't turn into another serial killer case," Carla muttered with a shake of her head.

Sara stared down at the victim. "Too soon to be saying that, but yes, I'm hoping it doesn't turn into one of those, too."

"One step at a time, ladies, let's not jump ahead of ourselves just yet."

"Any evidence around?"

"Nothing from what we can tell, except a few footprints. We've matched them to the victim."

"So the killer didn't even bother to check he was dead? Just kept shooting at him to make sure?" Sara scanned the area, looking for possible routes the killer could have taken.

Lorraine nodded. "Yep, that's what I figured." She bent down to turn the corpse over. "I suspect his heavy build would have hampered him in his plight to get away from his assailant."

"I think you're probably right." Sara took in the victim's hefty frame. "Are you sure there's no ID?"

"All his pockets were empty. No wallet, nothing in sight at all."

"Could the killer have robbed him and then forced him to run for his life?" Sara murmured as the cogs churned into action.

"It's possible. I'm not prepared to rule anything out at this stage."

Sara slammed her fists into her thighs. "If you only knew how much I hate these damn cases."

"Sorry, it wasn't intentional on my part, I can assure you. Maybe someone will ring the station and report him missing after a few days."

Sara peered through the trees at the sky beyond. "There's another flying pig. It's something we're gonna have to cling on to. Let's face it, it's all we have right now."

"Yeah, don't feel too bad about it. Let me do my thing this afternoon and get back to you with the results. You never know what might turn up during a PM."

"Okay, we'll leave it in your capable hands in that case. Or, we could attend the PM for a change. Carla, are you up for that?"

Carla rolled her eyes. "If we must."

"Well, that'll make a change, I must say," Lorraine ribbed them.

"Don't get used to it. This is a one-off, I'm not one of these DIs who get a thrill out of being involved that intimately in a case."

"I had noticed," Lorraine replied.

"Mind if Carla and I have a search around?"

"Be my guest. You know the rules, don't get too close to the victim."

"We'll do our best. Carla, let's head off this way. I want to see if there's anything down here worth looking into. Oh, by the way, Lorraine, who called it in?"

"A jogger. Says he jogs here every day. I've got a name and address for you. He was in a rush to get to work; he's a solicitor and had to be in court at ten this morning. I told him that you'd likely be in touch soon to take a statement. Did I do the right thing?"

"You did. I'll collect that information from you on the way back. See you soon."

Sara and Carla set off through the forest. If anything, the farther they travelled the denser it got.

"Shitting hell, this place is giving me the willies. It's a totally different atmosphere to Queenswood, isn't it?"

Carla shuddered. "Yeah, totally different prospect. Do you think that's why this place was chosen?"

"Possibly. There's no way of knowing that until we find the perp. Eerie as shit down here, though. If someone was chasing me with a gun, I'd be bricking it for sure."

"What kind of person hunts another down?"

Sara glanced behind her at Carla. "Someone with a grudge who has been wronged in the past, perhaps. Or, we could have a case not dissimilar to the numerous cases they've had in the US over the years, you know, where someone takes pot shots at folks."

Carla waved her head from side to side. "Maybe if he was out in the open, but here? What would he be doing here in the first place?"

"Fair point. Something we need to look into. What's bugging me is that there's no ID on the vic. It indicates that the killer is smart, aware of how we work."

"If you say so, although, every cop show on TV reveals what procedures are like nowadays, so I wouldn't necessarily bear any weight on that suggestion."

"I hear you. Frustrating all the same. Why can't we ever have an open-and-shut case fall into our laps occasionally?"

"The perps see it as a challenge to keep us on our toes."

"We'll need to contact the witness. Hopefully he can fill us in on a few details."

"I wouldn't hold out much hope on that one, although there's one thing in his favour."

"What's that?" Sara asked.

"He's 'in the trade' so to speak, so he should be more alert to these sorts of things than others."

"True enough. Let's get back, I'm freezing my tits off out here, even though it's twenty-two degrees today." Sara shivered, her teeth chattering slightly as they returned to the scene.

"Anything of note out that way?" Lorraine asked.

"Nothing as far as we can tell. Have you got the solicitor's details for us? We'll drop in on the way back to base."

Lorraine raised her eyebrows. "Aren't you forgetting one thing?"

Sara frowned and shrugged. "I don't think so, such as?"

"You're invited to take part in the PM today."

"I hadn't forgotten. You know me, I never go back on my word, no matter how tempting it might be. You tell us when and where and we'll be there."

"Okay. Let's say two this afternoon, is that all right with you guys?"

"Perfect. That gives us time to speak to the witness and to get the ball rolling with the rest of the team, not that we have much to go on yet."

"Hopefully that will change by the end of the day. Here's the witness's details. See you later."

Sara took the sheet of paper from Lorraine and smiled. "We'll be there." She removed her phone from her pocket and snapped off a few photos of the victim's puffy face full of cuts and abrasions.

## 2

Once they returned to the car, Carla rang the station to check with Missing Persons if they'd been notified about a person matching the victim's description while Sara stayed outside the car and contacted the witness's place of work.

"Hi, this is DI Sara Ramsey. Can you tell me when Christopher Downes will be free for a brief chat?"

"Oh, umm…let me check his appointment book. Ah, yes, he has a slot available after lunch, around two."

"Sorry, I'll be attending a post-mortem then. Any chance you can squeeze me in earlier? It should only take a few minutes, not a lengthy chat at all."

"He has to put his moniker on a will at midday, that shouldn't take him long to complete. Why don't you drop by then?"

"Fantastic. I'll do that. Thanks for your help."

"It's my pleasure."

Sara ended the call and let out a sigh of relief. She had imagined being kept on tenterhooks for days, waiting for his secretary to find a vacant slot. That was how it usually panned out with busy solicitors. She got in the car, and Carla was just ending her call. "Everything all right?"

"Yep, nothing as yet at their end. How did you get on?"

"They can fit us in around midday. The question is, what we do between now and then with no bloody ID available for the vic."

"Hmm…I hate these types of cases."

Sara turned over the engine and reversed the car, narrowly avoiding a large tree behind her. She eased her way back up the track to the main road, her gaze constantly darting around her. "If he was hunted, where did his assailant come from?"

"Pass."

"There are no obvious pathways through these woods, apart from this one, are there?"

"Not from what I can tell. Maybe the perp drove here and set the bloke loose with the intention of tracking him down."

"What if we're dealing with a bunch of people who get their kicks from chasing someone through the woods?"

"Where does that idea come from?"

Sara shrugged. "I don't know. Why does the perp always have to be working alone?"

"Fair point. I suppose we'll find out more after the PM. Talking of which, did you have to volunteer us for that one? You know how much I hate attending them."

Sara chuckled. "I know. I feel the same. We haven't gone to one in months. In fact, I can't remember the last one we did attend, can you?"

"Yep, which is why I prefer to swerve the task when at all possible." Carla heaved a little.

"Oh yes, I remember now. The last one was super gory and you spent most of the afternoon in the loo, right?"

"Don't remind me. Seeing a child cut open like that has to be the worst thing I've ever had to endure in my time on the force."

"Yeah, it wasn't pretty, from what I recall. Sorry, matey, that one had slipped my mind. You needn't come, if you don't want to."

"No, I should, you're right, it's all part of the service, so to speak, isn't it?"

"Yeah, we have to bite the bullet and dig deep into our emotional reserves to tackle the duties we hate the most now and again."

"Get you, that's very profound."

They both laughed. Sara drove back to the station. Once there, she brought the rest of the team up to date. She handed her phone to Carla and asked her to print off the image she'd taken of the victim which was then placed at the very top of the whiteboard, awaiting a name to sit alongside it. Then she went into her office to tackle some paperwork to while away the time. She detested being in limbo like this, with an unknown victim and nowhere to go to try to put a name to him. At eleven-thirty, she left her office, collected Carla once more and off they went. They arrived at the solicitor's at eleven-forty-five. The receptionist told them to take a seat. She buzzed through to Christopher Downes, but the man didn't emerge until over ten minutes later when he showed a client to the front door.

He turned to face them, his hand outstretched. "Sorry to keep you waiting, ladies. If you'd care to join me in my office."

They followed him into a neatly presented square room. The bookshelves behind his mahogany desk were packed to the ceiling with legal books, which appeared to be originals, in faded shades of green and orange. "Thanks for taking the time to see us, sir, we appreciate it. Perhaps you can tell us what you saw this morning?"

"Sorry, I can't talk to you at length, busy day on the appointment front. Not sure how I'm managing to switch off from what I stumbled across this morning, if I'm honest. It was such a shock, seeing that… man lying there. In all my years on this earth, that's thirty-eight by the way, I've never had the misfortune to be confronted by something as horrific as that. You don't expect it, not while you're engrossed in your morning run."

"I'm sorry you had to witness that, sir, it must have been very upsetting for you. Do you go for a run often in those woods?"

"Yes, virtually every day. I may vary it now and again but, well, it used to be my favourite haunt, if you like. Not sure I feel the same way about it now, though." He ran a hand through his black hair and glanced out of the small window, with its stark view out to the concrete back yard.

"It'll take time to get over the shock, sir."

He stared at Sara and nodded, his eyes sparkling with unshed tears. "You're not wrong there. I thought I was coping all right." He swiped at a stray tear which had dripped onto his cheek. "I guess we're never prepared when confronted with something as gruesome as that first thing. That poor man. Do you know who he is?"

"Not yet. We're going to have to use our detective skills on this one as there was no ID found on his body. I have to ask, did you see anyone else in the area?"

He shook his head and chewed on his lip. "No, in between my court case this morning and the other clients I've seen, I've tried to rack my brains, but unfortunately, I've drawn a blank."

"A possible vehicle perhaps?"

"Not from what I can remember. Bloody hell, I literally stumbled across his body in the woods. Did I disturb the scene?"

"We don't believe so. Did you happen to hear anything out of the ordinary?"

He gasped. "No. Are you suggesting the person who did this could have been watching me?"

Sara smiled. "I didn't mean to alarm you. It's not unheard of for perpetrators to hang around after they've killed someone."

"Why?" His gaze darted between Sara and Carla.

"Because of a morbid fascination they may have, who knows? I'm glad you weren't put in any immediate danger."

"Oh shit! What if the perp was out there, watching me, what if he comes after me next?"

"That's highly unlikely, Mr Downes. I'd advise you not to dwell on that too much."

"But you can't guarantee he won't, can you? Because you don't know who or what you're dealing with here, do you?"

"That's true. Please, try not to think about that. If you neither saw nor heard anything, then I'm sure there's no necessity for you to worry at all."

"I'll have to take your word on that one. I'll say this, I'm glad my diary is full today, otherwise the whole scenario would be playing over and over in my mind. Horrendous ordeal to be confronted with first thing in the morning, I can tell you."

"I'm sure. When was the last time you went for a run down there?"

"Yesterday. I've been running there on and off for a week or more."

"And you took the same route through the woods every day?"

"Yes. If you're asking if the body was there yesterday, I can assure you it wasn't, otherwise I would have reported it."

"Do you know if many people go there?"

"Hard to say really. I suppose other people must exercise down there, like I do. What form of exercise, I couldn't tell you. I see the odd jogger and dog walker on occasion. I tend to visit around seven, seven-thirty. I don't go there in the evening, not really, although I have been known to, you know, when I have to switch my schedule around. Jesus, sorry, now I'm waffling, aren't I? I'm nervous as hell. Is that normal?"

Sara smiled to try to reassure him. "Yes, perfectly normal in the circumstances. Well, if that's all you can tell us then we'll get out of your hair."

"What about giving you a proper statement, will you need one of those?"

"Would it be all right if we send a uniformed officer to see you in the next few days?"

He rose from his seat, and Sara and Carla followed him to the door.

"Yes, will they give me a call first?"

"Of course, we'll ensure that happens."

"Thanks. Sorry I wasn't much help. I hope you find the person responsible for this heinous crime. Give me a ring if you need to know anything else."

"We'll do that, Mr Downes. Thank you for squeezing us into your busy schedule." Sara handed him a card. "Give me a call if anything else comes to mind."

"I'll do that. Good luck." He opened the outer door for them and shook their hands again.

Sara noticed how slick his palm was, and once he closed the door, she wiped her hand down her trousers. "Yuck!"

Carla did the same before they got back in the car. "My thoughts exactly. Nice chap. Sad to see it's affected him like that."

"Yeah, you can tell he's never been in bother with the police before. Right, I suggest we grab a bite to eat somewhere. My treat, what do you fancy?"

Carla swiftly faced her. "Are you frigging mad? You know damn well what's on the agenda this afternoon."

"Okay, maybe the PM slipped my mind for a moment or two. Actually, I had a bigger breakfast than normal this morning, so perhaps I can afford to skip lunch after all."

"Lucky you, although I'd rather you not go into detail about what else goes on in your bedroom, thanks."

Sara chuckled. "You're an idiot at times. Right, what to do next? There lies the problem. Maybe I'm losing my touch at this policing lark."

"What the fuck are you talking about? What can we do when there's no frigging ID to the victim?"

"I know. It's at times like this I feel like a spare prick at a wedding, I can't help it."

"Let's go for a drink. I couldn't handle any food, knowing what's around the corner, but mulling things over while we sup a drink somewhere might get the brain cells working."

"Deal. I spotted a country pub around the corner, we'll stop there."

Sara pulled into the pub car park a few minutes later. The locals eyed them cautiously as they made their way to the bar.

The blonde barmaid smiled and asked, "What can I get you, ladies?"

"Two orange juice with ice, thanks." Sara paid for the drinks, and they wandered over to the table in the bay window, again under the scrutiny of the locals. Sara inclined her head and muttered, "I feel like the guys who visited that pub in *American Werewolf in London*."

"Jesus, how to put a girl on edge. Did you have to say that?" Carla glanced around, nervously smiling at the odd punter staring their way.

"Ignore them. Just raise your glass and say cheers."

Carla followed Sara's lead. "Bugger, I think we've just made matters worse. Looks like a few of them are talking about us now."

"Don't think about it. Let's concentrate on the case. Damn, wait a minute, my phone's ringing." She removed her mobile from her pocket and looked at the caller ID. It was her mother. "Sorry about this, it's Mum." She pressed the button. "Hi, Mum, how are you?"

"I'm well, love. I'm sorry to call you during the day, your father warned me not to but…"

"You're okay. What's wrong?"

"It's your brother, Timothy."

"Yeah, I know the one you mean, I've only got the one, Mum."

"Now, there's no need for you to be sarcastic. I wish I hadn't bothered ringing you now. Ignore me, go on, go about your day."

"Don't be silly. I was only joking. That's unusual of you not to twig that. What about Tim?"

"Well, I know you two don't get along, it's just that I'm worried about him. He usually checks in with us every couple of months, and I realised, whilst watching TV we haven't heard from him in some time."

"Meaning how long, Mum?"

"I tried to think last night. I believe it's at least three months, dear."

"Have you tried calling him?"

"Yes, there was no answer last night and, when I called again this morning, well, I got the same result. I'm worried about him. I know you're always extremely busy, but your father and I have got a lot on today, to do with church things and helping the needy in the community. Anyway, I digress, I was hoping you'd save us the job of trekking into town later to check on him. Would you go round there, Sara? If only to put my mind at rest?"

"Okay, things are a little slow today. I might be able to go there soon, although I have to be at a post-mortem at two."

"Oh my, did you have to mention that? My legs have started to shake now."

"You daft mare. It is what it is, Mum. Once someone dies that's the usual run of events."

"Dies, as in, murdered? Are you on another case, dear?"

"Yes, a body was discovered—"

"No, can I stop you there? I really don't want to know. I have enough on my plate being concerned about the starving people in our parish and what's going on with your brother right now. I'm not sure I can handle anything else as sinister as listening to another one of your investigations."

"That's a bit OTT even for you, Mum. Okay, I'll spare you the details. I'll probably visit Tim after the PM, I'll have more time then."

"As you will, thank you. I appreciate you going out of your way to see your least favourite person."

"I'm doing it for you and Dad, remember that the next time you slate me for losing touch with my brother, won't you?"

"I will. Let me know how things go. Thank you, Sara."

"You're welcome. I'll be in touch soon. Gotta go." She stabbed at the 'end call' button and slammed her phone on the table. Several punters sitting close by snapped their heads in her direction. She grinned and bared her teeth at them. "Sorry. Domestic trouble. As you were, folks."

"Is your mum okay?"

"She wants me to check in on my useless brother."

"You've never really spoken about him. What gives?"

"He's a waste of space most of the time. His marriage broke up a few years ago, and he sought solace in a bottle. He's vile and offensive, and I detest being around him. Mark's never met him, I refuse to introduce them."

"Ah, I see, the black sheep of the family. We've all got one."

"Have you? Who's that?"

"My uncle, Lennie. He went off with a scarlet woman."

"No. Was she a lady of the night?" Sara asked, intrigued.

Carla waved a hand. "Yes, I really don't want to go there. It ripped our family apart when they took off. Anyway, I need to know what's going on with your brother."

"I wish I knew. We used to be really close growing up; he's my older brother. It all changed when he married his wife. He thought I interfered too much in their marriage, I seem to recall. I didn't, not in the slightest. How could I when I was based up in Liverpool and he lived down here? Anyway, I got the impression he blamed me for the breakdown of his marriage. That's when he turned to drink and his vicious tongue started up. When Philip died, he didn't show me an ounce of sympathy. Even took me to one side and slurred out the words that he thought Philip had had a lucky escape dying on me like that."

"He said *what*? That's so unfair, unkind of him to say that. I'm not surprised you've turned your back on him."

"It was the last straw. I've tried my best to support him over the years, but to say that, well, it felt like a dagger to the heart, I can tell you. Bastard!"

"Does your mum know why you fell out with him?"

"No, I've kept it from my parents. I couldn't hurt them. They adore him, Lord knows why. Mum is under the impression that I hate his drinking habits."

"Blimey! And there was me thinking you had the perfect family, well, apart from Philip's mother and her vicious tongue, which you've had to deal with the past few years."

"Yeah, thankfully, I think Charlotte has finally got the message and has decided to leave me alone now."

"That's great news. Must be a relief, what with the wedding coming up. I had a feeling she was going to show up on the day and cause a problem for you and Mark."

"I thought the same, I must admit."

"Going back to your brother, do you want to drop in on him now? We've got enough time."

"No, let the bastard wait. We'll have this, bounce a few ideas around and then go see Lorraine."

"Ideas? You're optimistic. Do you have any at this point?" Carla sipped her drink.

"Not really. Only that if the victim was deliberately hunted down then my guess would be the perp was on some kind of revenge trip. I could be way off the mark with that assumption, so don't listen to me. I suppose we'll be floundering until we can ID him, as frustrating as that sounds. One thing is for certain, having a victim who has been deliberately hunted on our patch isn't sitting comfortably with me."

"I agree. It's almost creepy." Carla shuddered, glanced around her at the other punters and lowered her voice. "A bit like being here, amongst this mob."

"Yeah, I hear you. Try not to let them intimidate you. Ignore them if you can."

"Pretty hard when they're all gawping at us like we're rabid caged animals or something."

Sara sniggered. "There is that. Come on, pay attention." She nudged Carla's knee with her own, and Carla shrieked.

"Jesus, did you have to do that? You scared the crap out of me."

"I said ignore them. Okay, let's finish our drinks and get on the road. We'll take a leisurely drive over to the mortuary; at least the scenery is more desirable on this side of the town."

"One thing in our favour at least."

They left their table and crossed the room to the main door.

"The freak show is over now, chaps. Thanks for the warm welcome. Maybe we'll come back in a day or two with the drug squad to see what you folks are buying from behind the bar along with your pints." Sara turned her back on the crowd amidst shocked gasps and shouts of "Here, you can't say that!" and "Who the hell do you think you are?"

Once they were in the safety of the car again, they both burst into laughter.

"Crikey, you stirred up a bag of shit there," Carla said.

Sara shrugged. "That'll teach them to be so off-hand with visitors. And they wonder why dozens of pubs are closing their doors at the moment through lack of bloody trade. I ask you, we were as welcome in that place as the thousands of rats invading their cellars."

Carla slapped her hands over her face and shook her head. "Jesus, did you have to conjure up such an image? I bloody hate rats."

"I can't say they're my best buddies either. Buckle up, we're out of here." She engaged the engine and switched on the radio, hoping to catch the news.

They pulled up outside the hospital around thirty minutes later, long before they were supposed to. Sara took a punt it would be okay and they entered the bowels of the hospital. An involuntary shiver tickled the length of her spine. This place always had that effect on her, which was probably why she avoided it so much. They found Lorraine going through some paperwork in her office.

She looked up as they entered and immediately took note of the clock on the wall. "Umm...didn't I say two?"

"You did. We got bored, you know, with a lack of leads to follow up on. I was wondering if we could persuade you to tackle the PM early."

Lorraine bounced back in her chair and spread her arms wide. "Just because you haven't got any useful work you can throw yourself into, that doesn't go for the rest of us. As you can see, my paperwork will likely keep me amused, and I use the term sarcastically, for at least two years."

"Sorry, I just thought you might be as eager as us to get it out of the way." Sara smiled broadly at her pathologist friend.

Lorraine wagged a finger. "Don't go thinking you can charm me on this one, DI Ramsey. I have a schedule of my own to keep, you know."

"Okay, but..."

Lorraine threw her hands up in the air. "I know when I'm beat. Anything for a bloody easy life. Come on, tog up. The quicker I can get you two out from under my feet the better." She breezed past Sara and Carla and stormed up the strongly lit hallway.

Sara pumped the air, and Lorraine shouted over her shoulder, "I saw that. Don't think you've won this round, Ramsey."

"What? I didn't do anything." Sara fought hard to restrain the urge to giggle.

The three of them entered the locker room, and Lorraine sorted through a pile of green scrubs and threw a couple of suitable ones in their direction.

"They should fit you. I'll go on ahead. Give me five minutes to get the body ready, if that's not too much to ask." After tugging on her scrubs, she exited the room again.

"Why do you persist in pissing her off like that?" Carla slipped her top over her head and straightened her hair before pulling on the elasticated cap.

"I wasn't aware I had. It wasn't my intention. She's super strung out lately. I need to find time to take her out on the town, uncover what's going on that's making her so touchy."

"Good luck with that one, not sure how you're going to fit it into your busy schedule."

"Me neither. Are you ready?"

"Yep, almost. Just got to source a pair of these vile calf-height wellies."

After locating the correct footwear, they found Lorraine preparing the corpse in her theatre.

"Ah, ladies, don't be shy, come closer."

"We were hoping you would've made the incisions by now and already pulled back the skin. That's the part that gets to me the most."

"Is it?" Lorraine displayed her pearly white teeth. "I would never have guessed. It's true what they say, revenge is very sweet indeed. That'll teach you to piss me off in the future, right?"

Sara groaned. "You can go off some people, you know. And there was me singing your praises to my partner and telling her that I need to take you out for a drink soon. Well, you can forget that idea. Go on then, get on with it."

Sara and Carla looked away while the Y-incision was cut into the corpse.

The detectives kept quiet while Lorraine ran through her procedures and findings for the purposes of the recording. "There are several gunshot wounds to the upper torso. One entered the heart. There is no exit wound at the back, therefore, I'm presuming that once I cut the heart open, I'll find the evidence which will lead us to the COD. The victim has a bullet wound to his right thigh, which has an entry and exit wound. Also, on the hip, there's another bullet wound—no exit hole there, though. Moving back to the torso, there are three bullet entry wounds—nicks, if you will—to the sides as if these were the perpetrator's initial shots fired."

"They weren't good, so he was perfecting his skills, is that what you're suggesting?" Sara asked quietly.

Lorraine nodded. "So it would appear. I can't see any other wounds on the body, nothing of note anyway that would suggest another implement had been used."

"Phew, that's a relief. Well, sort of," Sara mumbled.

"There are no ligature marks on his wrists or his ankles…no, wait, I can see a slight abrasion on his wrists. My interpretation is that he was possibly bound by rope, and yet there was no evidence of any bindings found at the murder scene."

"Could they have dropped off during his exertions, you know, him running?" Sara enquired.

"Maybe. A more likely scenario is that the killer removed the bindings and took them with him, to hide any trace evidence or DNA from us."

"Makes sense. Any wounds to his head?"

Lorraine took a few moments to examine it closely and nodded. "Yes, there appears to be a couple of bumps, one on either side. Perhaps the perpetrator knocked him out initially to abduct him, who knows? Okay, that concludes the external examination. I'm going in. Are you two going to be all right with this part?"

Sara and Carla nodded.

"Then I'll begin. Let's start with the heart." She removed it from the cavity and sliced it open. Something metallic hit the tray as Lorraine placed the organ in it. She dug around underneath the heart and said, "Aha, as suspected. Here's the culprit which I believe took his life. I'll get that off to the lab for them to analyse it."

"Can you ask them to rush the results through for me?"

"I can try, depends how backed up they are."

"Okay, something is better than the nothing we're working with right now. You mentioned there was no exit wound to the hip as well, could there be another bullet there?"

Lorraine looked up at the ceiling as she dug around in the man's flesh. "Here we are, another bullet to add to our collection."

"Can you tell if the bullets are from the same gun?"

"I'd rather not try and predict that. Let's leave that to the experts, I've been known to be wrong in the past."

"Fair enough. Can I have a look, just to satisfy myself?" Sara stepped forward, cringing a little at the intense smell the closer she got to the corpse.

Lorraine wiped the bullets clean as best she could on a nearby cloth and placed them in separate dishes for Sara to inspect.

"My opinion would be they're from the same gun, but we'll wait for the confirmation. If they are from the same weapon, that's a good thing, at least we know that only one gun was used and the attack was likely carried out by one assailant."

"I'm inclined to agree with you, however, I'm not committing myself just yet. Let's see what the lab has to say first. Their tests can pick up things the naked eye can't see, such as odd striations on the casings."

"I'm aware of that," Sara noted.

"Good. Let's get on, see what other facts this young man can tell us." Lorraine reached inside the corpse again and extracted the stomach. "Get me the largest tray you can find, there, no, over there, that one should do."

Sara dashed across the room and returned with a white tray made from robust plastic. She placed it on the spare metal trolley next to Lorraine and watched the pathologist slice the stomach open. The contents spilled out and filled Sara's nostrils with a vile aroma of mixed smells. "Jesus, that's obscene."

"You could say that," Carla agreed, heaving.

"If you're going to be sick, leave the room," Lorraine shouted, the colour draining from Carla's face at the sight laid out in front of her. "Okay, we've got a final meal of what appears to be fish and chips."

"Not forgetting the mushy peas." Sara pointed at the green pellets floating in the excess liquid.

"I think you'll find they're normal peas," Lorraine proposed, and she moved a few of them over to one side. "These are still whole as opposed to being mush. He obviously wasn't one for chewing his food much."

"I bow to your superior knowledge." Sara grinned. "Can you tell when he ate his last meal?"

"A guesstimate would be within the last ten hours or thereabouts."

"What's that brown liquid? I'm guessing it's either beer or lager, yes?"

"I'd say you were correct. I'm getting a distinct smell of hops."

"So, the killer either gave him his last meal of fish and chips washed down with several pints, judging by the amount swimming there, or he likely picked up the victim after he'd been on a night out. Or am I reading too much into it?" Sara said.

"Bravo, that's the same assumption I've made. You're getting good at this detecting lark," Lorraine quipped.

"Well, it's something. More than we had when we first arrived. Anything else, Lorraine?"

"Not from what I can see. If you want to hang around for a bit longer, I can slice up the liver and kidneys for you. My guess is they're going to be fattier organs than I normally have to deal with, judging by the man's weight. And no, that's not a body-shaming statement, it's a bloody factual one."

"We'll give it a miss if you don't mind. Send me the results ASAP if you will." Sara was already heading towards the door.

Carla followed and muttered, "Thank fuck for that. I've got bile burning my damn throat. Good luck, Lorraine, I couldn't do your job."

"Not many people have the stomach for it, that's for sure. Thanks for your company, ladies. I'll be in touch soon."

Sara and Carla changed swiftly, went for a pee, and then left the building. "Is it any wonder we hate attending damn PMs? I feel lousy, in dire need of a shower. I fear the stench is going to linger on my skin the rest of the day."

"Yep, it's all too much for me. I almost puked when Lorraine opened his stomach. How gross was that?"

"The bloody pits. I'm sure she did some of that on purpose, just to get a rise out of us, she's warped like that. I wouldn't put it past her to toy with our mental state."

"You think?" Carla slipped into the passenger seat.

Sara inhaled a large breath of fresh air and entered the car. Her mobile rang. "Bloody hell, it's my mother."

"Oops, it has been a few hours, I suppose," Carla noted.

"Hi, Mum." Sara tried to keep her tone light.

"Hello, love, any news for us yet? I'm sorry to keep bugging you, I appreciate how busy you are trying to solve a murder case, it's just that…well, you know."

"We've only just left the PM, Mum. We're on our way over to Tim's flat now. I'll get back to you soon if I have any news worth sharing, okay?"

"Oh, thank you, love, bless you. I'm so sorry for pestering you."

"There's no need to apologise. Speak later."

Sara ended the call and puffed out her cheeks. "Ever in demand, no matter what time of day, eh? You don't mind stopping off, do you?"

"Why should I? Go for it. It's not like we've got our backs against the wall on this one, not yet anyway."

"Thanks. I'll be in and out. Ha, he'll probably kick me out before I have the option of leaving, knowing Tim. I can't say I'm looking forward to seeing him again, not after falling out with him."

"Grit your teeth, put a smile on your face and you'll be all right. Where does he live?"

"Not too far, around five minutes, close to the city centre, within staggering distance of the nightlife Hereford has to offer an alcoholic. Harsh but true as they say."

Several minutes later, Sara was climbing the stairs to the block of flats overlooking the River Wye running through the centre of the city. She'd assured Carla she could do the trip alone and left her partner in the car, contacting the station, giving the team a quick update.

Out of breath, kicking herself for not using the damn lift, Sara reached the seventh floor where her brother resided. She knocked on the door and stood back. There was no answer.

*Shit! Don't say I've had a wasted bloody trip. Answer the damn door if you're in there and not slumped over a chair in a drunken stupor, arsehole!*

She knocked again, louder this time.

A woman poked her head out of the next-door flat. "I haven't seen or heard from him in days, a rarity, I can tell you."

"I see. Is he usually noisy then?"

"Yep, the more I complain the worse he gets. Ignorant fucking bastard. I've got a two-year-old in here who's better behaved than that twazzock."

"Sorry to hear that."

"What do you want from him? I'm right in thinking you're the filth —sorry, the police—aren't I?"

"You are. Although this is a social visit. He's a relative of mine."

"Shit! Bad luck for you. He's a horrible man. I've met him on the stairs a few times during the week, always paralytic, out of his head, going from one side of the stairs to the other, doing it on purpose I shouldn't wonder."

"Oh dear. Sounds like Tim, he does have a stubborn streak."

"No kidding. My boyfriend has threatened to teach him a lesson on more than one occasion, I can tell you, most of the men around here have. He's pig-ignorant and couldn't give a toss about the community. We're decent folks living here, it's not a rough part of town, not like some I could mention, and yet we're stuck with the likes of him living on our doorstep. Oh God, I swore I wouldn't let him rile me again. See what the bastard stirs up in me?"

Sara shrugged. "He's not the best person to get on with, years of experience on my side will tell you that. I'll knock again. Can you pinpoint exactly when you last saw him?"

The neighbour placed a thumb and forefinger around her chin. "Hmm…bin day is Monday, I don't recall him putting his out this week. I might be mistaken, though, the little one has had a poorly tummy all week, bless her, so I'm getting all my days mixed up."

"Thanks for the insight. Sorry to hear about your child, maybe a trip to the doctor's is called for."

"I went. They sent me off to the pharmacy to see what they had to treat it. Waste of time going to the doctor's, if you ask me."

"Sorry to hear that."

"It's inconvenient either way, it's not like I'm sat at home all day on benefits like some scallies. I'm a single working mum. I refuse to bleed the nation dry like some I could mention. I hope you get a response soon. Have you tried ringing him? Or is that a dumb question?"

"No, it's not dumb. My mother has. She was concerned about him and asked me to check in on him as I was in town. Enjoy the rest of your day. Thanks for your help."

"Good luck." The neighbour closed her front door again, and Sara bashed on Tim's once more.

Annoyingly, there was no response. She crouched and peered through the letterbox. What she hadn't expected was the stench that hit her. *Jesus, Tim! It smells like a bloody distillery.* At least, that was her first observation. She stood, inhaled a clean breath of fresh air and tried again. This time she encountered an entirely different smell that shot alarm bells ringing throughout her whole system.

Stepping away from the front door, she rang Carla's mobile. Her partner answered immediately.

"Sara? What's up?"

"I need you up here. *Now.*" Sara ended the call, her voice quivering with the shock rampaging through her body.

Carla arrived five minutes later, her brow wrinkled with sweat and confusion. "What's going on? Is it Tim?" she asked breathlessly.

"I want you to look through the letterbox."

"What?"

"No questions, just do it. Tell me what you find."

Carla grumbled under her breath but did as instructed. She crouched and opened the letterbox. Pretty soon she stumbled backwards, placing her hands on the concrete landing to steady herself. "Jesus, Sara, that's not right."

"I needed your corroboration. I need to break the door down and get in there."

Carla jumped to her feet and rubbed Sara's arm to comfort her. "I'll call for backup. Hang in there."

Sara's gaze was fixed on the front door of the flat, and she drifted off. In the background, Carla's voice remained calm as she rang the station for assistance, and then they had to wait another ten minutes before help arrived in the form of two uniformed officers carrying an Enforcer or what they called 'a big red key'.

Sara and Carla stood back. The door gave way at the first attempt. Then the officers stood aside to allow Sara and Carla to enter the flat. Sara tried to brace herself for what lay ahead, but her nerves overwhelmed her and her legs failed to move forward. Carla swept past her and took the lead.

"Shit! Sara, don't come in here."

It was too late, she'd already summoned up the strength from somewhere to enter the room. "Oh God! The fucking stench…no, don't tell me he's…"

"You shouldn't be in here. You don't need to see him like this, love."

Carla stepped forward and tried to usher her away, but Sara refused to budge an inch. This was her brother, the one who had looked out for her all those years ago when she'd been bullied at school by a bunch of older lads. The brother who had helped her with her maths homework when she'd lagged behind in class because the student teacher had lost control and didn't know how to handle the sixth formers he was supposed to be teaching in readiness for their exams. The same brother who had turned on her in recent years, since his marriage had failed and his kids had been taken away from him. Her heart was breaking now. Years of uncertainty about what was going on with him and now to be confronted with this, it all proved to be too much. Carla slung an arm around her shoulder and guided her to the chair farthest away from Tim who was sprawled out on the floor amongst the overturned furniture.

She had enough procedural sense to warn Carla not to move anything. "We need to get SOCO here, something doesn't feel right to me."

"In what way?" Carla asked. She took in her surroundings and shrugged.

"This isn't him. I mean, it's him, and I know he was an alcoholic, but finding him like this, I can't believe what I'm seeing."

"Okay, should we leave the flat, if that's what you're suggesting?"

Sara rose to her feet and swayed a little. "Yes, let's get out of here."

Once outside, she dismissed the two uniformed officers but then thought better of it. "No, stay. You need to cordon off this level. Don't let anyone in or out, not until SOCO give us the nod, you hear me?"

The officers nodded and raced back to their car to fetch the crime scene tape. Sara watched them over the balcony while Carla rang the station and instructed the girl on control to arrange for SOCO to attend the scene.

"They'll be here soon. Stupid question, how are you holding up?"

"I'm okay, I think. Fuck! What am I going to tell my parents? Mum's expecting me to call her, I can't tell her this over the phone."

"Too right. You're going to have to do it in person. Better still, I should be the one to do that, you shouldn't be involved in the case, you know that, Sara. God, what a mess, I'm so sorry for your loss."

Sara buried her head in her hands, and the tears fell at last. "Jesus, why him? Why did he have to die like that?"

"It's best not to dwell on it, Sara. We'll get to the bottom of it."

"I need to call the chief, make her aware of the situation. I need someone I can trust to take over this case." She fished her phone out of her pocket and rang the station. Mary, the chief's secretary, came on the line. "Mary, it's Sara Ramsey, I need to speak to DCI Price right away."

"I think she's free. Hold the line, Sara."

She drummed her fingers on the concrete balcony.

"DI Ramsey, what's the problem?"

"Sorry to trouble you, ma'am, I need a favour."

"What sort of favour?"

"It's my brother…well, he's dead. Carla and I are here now. The thing is, I think it's a suspicious death. We're awaiting SOCO. I know I can't take the case on…"

"You want me to appoint someone capable of investigating the case thoroughly, is that it?"

"Yes, ma'am."

"Damn! My condolences, Sara. What a shock for you to find him like that."

"It was. Can you arrange someone to take over ASAP? I need to get to my parents, to break the news."

"Of course. Leave it with me, I'll get on it straight away. Hang in there!"

"I will. Thanks, boss." Sara ended the call and immediately rang Lorraine's personal mobile.

Breathlessly, the pathologist answered in her usual bright tone. "Hey, you, did you forget something?"

"Are you busy?"

"Not really, except for writing up your report. What's wrong?"

"I need you here. It's…well…shit, why is this so hard to bloody say?" Her voice broke.

"Just say it, Sara, you're scaring me. What's wrong?"

"It's my brother, he's dead. I want you to take care of him, no one else will do, Lorraine."

"Fuck! I'm there, tell me where I need to be, I'll be there soon."

"Thank you." Sara handed the phone to Carla. "Can you tell her where to come?"

She rubbed the tears away from her eyes, sick to death of them clouding her vision. Thoughts of breaking the news to her parents and her sister, Lesley, filled her with dread. She'd have to go there soon. She'd wait to see what Lorraine had to say first, though.

"Are you all right?" Carla gave her phone back to her.

"I don't think I'll ever be all right again. I know he was a cantankerous bastard, but he was still my flesh and blood, no matter how I paint it. Mum is going to be traumatised by this. She had a bloody feeling something was wrong. Neither of us expected this outcome, I'm sure."

"Is Lorraine on her way?"

"Yep, she should be here soon. Christ, I know it's not the best thing to say in the circumstances, but I could do with a bloody brandy."

"I feel for you. I'm at a loss to find the right words to comfort you."

"Just being here helps, don't feel bad."

"Want a hug?"

"Not unless you fancy a soggy shoulder. I'm fine. It's my parents I'm worried about."

"You should ring Mark, maybe he'll go with you to see them."

"Christ! I forgot all about Mark." She rang the vet's, and he was in between patients.

"Hi, anything wrong, sweetheart?"

"Hi, you could say that. I'm at my brother's. Mum was worried about him, so I dropped by to see if he was all right."

"And is he?"

"No, Mark, he's dead!"

"What? Bloody hell, how? Are you all right?"

"We don't know how. The place stinks of booze. The neighbour said she hadn't seen or heard him for a few days. Lord knows how long he's been lying here while we've all been getting on with our lives, not bothering what was going on with him."

"Stop that! Don't you dare go blaming yourself for this, Sara. He's not been the easiest man to get on with lately. I won't allow you to feel guilty, you hear me?"

"I hear you. It's not going to make a scrap of difference, though. I'm waiting for the pathologist and another inspector to turn up and then I'll shoot over to see Mum and Dad."

"Do you want me to shuffle appointments around and come with you?"

"No. Don't do that. I'm sure I'll be fine. Carla will be with me."

"Okay, ring me if you need anything. My condolences, love. I'll see you later."

"Thanks. See you tonight."

"I love you."

"Me, too. Bye."

The roar of a motorbike entering the car park drew her attention. Lorraine stepped off the machine and removed her helmet. She balanced it on the seat of her bike and shook out her scarlet hair. Sara waved. Lorraine gave her the thumbs-up, grabbed her medical bag out of the storage box and made her way up to them.

She hugged Sara the second she was within reach. "I'm so sorry. Are you all right?"

"I'm holding up. Thanks for coming, I truly appreciate it."

"I would have been upset if you hadn't rung me. Is he inside?"

"Yep, in all his glory. I'm coming in with you."

"Do you think that's wise?"

"I need to find out how he died, Lorraine. I'd rather you tell me than some jumped-up prick of an inspector who knows fuck all about me and my family."

"Okay. We need to get suited up first."

"Have you got two spare sets in your bag?"

"Only the one."

"Carla, can you fetch another set from the boot of my car?"

Carla nodded and set off. "I won't be a tick."

"Now she's out of the way, you can level with me. How are you, really?" Lorraine asked.

"Apart from being riddled with guilt, I just feel numb. I'm dreading telling my folks the news."

"Can't you leave it for the inspector taking over the investigation?"

Sara shook her head. "Are you crazy?"

Carla returned a few minutes later, and the three of them togged up and entered the flat together. Lorraine assessed the crime scene from afar and then stepped close to Tim. She moved the collar of his open shirt and revealed a large gash in his neck.

"He had his throat cut? He couldn't have done that himself, could he?" Sara asked.

"Possibly, but highly unlikely. And no, it wasn't enough to cause him any real discomfort. I fear it looks worse than it is."

"So, how did he die?"

Lorraine pulled up her brother's sleeve and stared up at her. "Did you know he was a user?"

Sara let out a huge sigh. "I didn't have a clue. Shit! The stupid bastard, what the hell was wrong with him? How could he do this to Mum and Dad?"

"Oi, let's not jump to conclusions just yet. There are tests we can do, to work out how long he's been using. Let's not forget this is a suspicious death."

"You think someone did this to him?" Sara asked, shocked by Lorraine's revelation.

"I'm just erring on the side of caution for now. If you said he wasn't using then that seems the obvious answer to me."

"Okay, who? Why? How did they get in here?"

"Any signs of forced entry?"

Sara glanced at Carla. "We didn't check, apart from the obvious, of course, us breaking down the door to gain entry."

"My guess is that either he let them in or they forced their way past him, possibly when he opened the door. All supposition at this point. I take it you've had a word with the neighbours?"

"I had a brief chat. She didn't mention hearing a recent ruckus. I can ask the neighbour on the other side, if that will help?"

"Or we could leave all that to the inspector," Carla pointed out.

A male entered the flat. "Good idea. What are you doing here? As far as I'm aware this investigation has my name on it."

As soon as Sara saw who the voice belonged to, she cringed. *Damn Luke Renshaw!*

"Hello, Luke. Nice of you to come." Sara held out her hand for him to shake.

He ignored it. "Just answer the question, Ramsey."

"Didn't DCI Price tell you?"

"Nope. She said nothing, just told me to get over here ASAP. Now, mind telling me why there are two inspectors here?"

Sara sighed. "The victim is my brother."

"Whoa! Now, Inspector, you know the rules as well as I do, you shouldn't be here. Outside with you, pronto." He gestured at the door with his chin.

Resigned to the fact he was right about the protocol in this instance, Sara motioned for Carla to leave with her. She stopped in front of

*Run For Your Life*

Renshaw and poked a finger in his chest. "If I hear you're slacking on this investigation, you'll have me to deal with, got that?"

"Idle threats don't wash with me, Inspector. I suggest you go back to the station and get on with the case already appointed to you."

"I'll do that after I've broken the news to my parents," she said defiantly.

"That's not advisable."

"I couldn't give a toss. I'm doing it, and no one is going to stop me." She turned and walked away.

Carla followed her up the hallway. "Was that wise? Ticking him off like that?"

"Wise or not, it's done now. I hope Lorraine gives him hell as well."

Renshaw's voice followed them to the front door. "I know you two are friends, but I'm asking you, no, I'm telling you, to keep Ramsey out of this investigation, am I making myself clear?"

Sara turned, ready to go back in there and belt Renshaw, but Carla tussled with her and shoved her out of the front door.

"Oh no you don't. Leave him to get on with it. You're risking your career if you interfere, Sara, you know that."

"Okay, you win. I'm warning you now, if he screws up, he's gonna have me to deal with, and I won't hold back."

"He knows that. Give him a chance."

Sara stomped the length of the balcony and hopped on the lift. She didn't say another word to Carla until they reached the car. "I'd better ring my sister, ask her to be there as well."

"Okay."

She withdrew her phone from her pocket, hand shaking. "Hi, Lesley. Are you busy?"

"No, not really. I'm on the way to Mum and Dad's with a tray of eggs I promised to pick up for them. What's wrong?"

"Okay, I'm on my way out there, too. I'll see you soon."

"That sounds ominous."

"See you later." She hung up before her sister could say anything else.

"Do you want me to drive, to give you a break?" Carla offered.

"No, I'll be fine. Thanks for being so thoughtful."

"Anytime."

They stepped out of their protective suits, placed them in evidence bags and handed them to one of the uniformed coppers with strict instructions to give them to SOCO. Sara was lost in thought and slotted into autopilot during the drive out to Marden. Heaving out a large sigh, she announced, "We're here. Do you want to stay in the car? I know how much you hate this side of things."

"Are you kidding me? No, I want to be by your side, supporting you."

Sara issued a weak smile; it was an effort. "You're amazing. I couldn't wish for a better partner. Come on then, let me introduce you to my folks."

Carla reached out and squeezed Sara's hand for a moment. "At your own pace, remember that."

"Thanks, I'll try not to forget that."

They left the vehicle and approached the garden gate. Sara waved at her mother who was peering out of the front window.

"Oh shit! She looks so hopeful, and before long I'm going to be seen as the bad guy."

Carla tutted. "You're reading too much into this. She won't blame you, how can she?"

"We'll see. Brace yourself for a lot of tears." Sara used her key to gain access to the house.

Her mother was standing in the hallway, clinging to the lounge doorframe.

*Sod it! Lesley isn't here yet!*

"Hi, Mum. This is my partner, Carla, you've heard me mention her a few times over the years."

"Hello, Carla. Wonderful to meet you, finally. Well, did you go and see him? Tim? I'm guessing you did otherwise you wouldn't be here. You would have rung us. Come on, is he all right? Was he drunk again?"

"Let's go through to the lounge. Where's Dad?"

"He's out back in the potting shed. Is it serious?" Her mother's hand shook as she touched her face.

"Carla, I'll get Dad, if you can settle Mum in the lounge. I won't be long."

Carla nodded and guided Sara's mother back into the lounge.

Sara raced through to the kitchen and rang her sister. "Lesley, where are you?"

"Just pulling up now. What's the great urgency?"

"See you in a moment." She ended the call and ventured out into the garden.

Her father backed out of the shed, carrying a tray of tomato plants.

"Hi, Dad."

"Ugh…you nearly scared me to death, child. What on earth?"

"I'm sorry. Can you come inside, there's something I need to tell you."

Her father followed her into the kitchen at the same time the front door opened, and in walked Lesley carrying a tray of eggs.

"Wow, this is a surprise, seeing you here during the day, Sara. What gives?" Lesley asked, playing along.

"Hey, I'm glad you're here. I have something to tell you all. Pop them down and come through to the lounge."

Lesley's brow furrowed. "Okay, two secs."

After her father had washed and dried his hands and announced he was ready, Sara hooked her arm through his and went into the lounge where they found Sara's mother interrogating Carla about her wedding plans.

"That's enough about that, wishing you and your young man every happiness for the future, Carla. We can't wait for Sara and Mark to tie the knot. The whole family is excited. Oh my, Lesley, I thought I heard you come in. What are you doing here?"

Her sister crossed the room and kissed her mother on the top of her head. "Hi, Mum, I brought a tray of eggs for you." She perched on the arm of her mother's chair.

"Well, it's lovely to see you both and to make Carla's acquaintance, but would someone mind telling me the real reason behind you all showing up here like this?"

Sara sat next to Carla on the couch and patted the seat beside her. "Sit here, Dad."

Her father groaned as he flopped into his seat. "Damn bones will be the death of me. Old and decrepit, that's me. Sorry, Carla, you don't want to hear about my aches and pains." He smiled at her.

"It's fine. It comes to us all in the end." Carla smiled at Sara's father then glanced at Sara and nodded, giving her the go-ahead to begin.

Sara clenched her hands together until her knuckles turned white. "Okay, I'm glad you're all here. I have something to tell you and, well, it's not going to be easy."

Her mother gasped, and she clutched Lesley's hand. "It's Tim, please tell me nothing bad has happened to him."

"Sorry, Mum." Sara unclenched her hands and placed one on top of her father's. "Carla and I called in to see him not long ago and…oh God, this has to be one of the hardest things I've ever had to tell you. I'm sorry, but Tim's dead."

"What?" her father shouted, snatching his hand away.

"Please, Dad, hear me out."

"Dead! How?" her mother whispered, the colour quickly draining from her cheeks.

Lesley sat there in silence, shaking her head in disbelief.

"I've had to call in a colleague to take over the investigation. We're unsure what the cause of death is at this stage. I'm so sorry."

Tears streamed down her mother's face, and Lesley comforted her. Sara stared at her father; his gaze was drawn to the window. He swallowed as if trying his hardest to force back the tears. Maybe he would have reacted differently if Carla hadn't been there.

"Shall I make some tea?" Carla asked.

Sara nodded. "Thanks, love, a coffee for me and Lesley, if you would."

Carla swept out of the room.

"Say something, Mum."

Between sobs, her mother said, "What is there to say? I've lost a child, my only son. I know he wasn't perfect, but he was my child all the same. Why would he die at his age?"

"We've yet to determine that, Mum. Please don't put yourself through this."

"Why, why didn't I contact him more often? She's to blame, leaving him the way she did and taking his beautiful children away from him. I'll never forgive her, ever."

"We don't know what really went on between them, Mum, he didn't really confide in any of us, did he? He's always been a bit of a loner."

"Not in the beginning. *She* changed him. The minute those two got married, well, he seemed to cut us out of his life."

"That's not true," Lesley replied. "You can't blame her for his misgivings, Mum. He chose to drown his sorrows rather than reach out for help. We would have bent over backwards for him, done anything for him, had he asked either one of us. Instead, it was his decision to cut us out of his life."

"We shouldn't have allowed it, Lesley. We should have all been more supportive in his hour of need."

"That's a bit unfair, Mum," Sara jumped in. "How can you help someone who refuses to speak to you? Who turns his back on you?"

Her mother glared at her. "That's your perception. You gave up on him easier than the rest of us, and yet, you were the closest to him in your younger years."

"That's totally unjust." She lowered her head and mumbled, "I was grieving the loss of my husband. Struggling with my own emotional well-being."

Carla entered the room carrying a tray with five mugs on it. She set it down on the coffee table. "I wasn't sure if any of you took sugar, so I brought the cannister in to help yourselves."

Sara smiled. "Thanks."

"And there lies the problem," her mother said, taking up where she left off. "Maybe if we hadn't put all our efforts into getting you back on track, perhaps Tim wouldn't have felt such an outcast. His marriage broke down around the same time as Philip was buried, didn't it?"

"I think so. Bad timing. None of us could have foreseen this happening, Mum. When I got married, I thought it would be for life. We all have to overcome certain situations and dilemmas that steer our lives off course at one time or another, don't we?"

"True enough, Sara," her father said, finally finding his voice. "This is a sad time, however, I don't think it's a time for recriminations. Tim was his own person, who genuinely preferred his own company. There was little any of us could have done to alter that. It is what it is. He's gone now. How did you find him?"

"I had to call for backup to break down the door. He was lying on the floor, surrounded by empty bottles."

"Are you insinuating that he drank himself to death?" her sister demanded.

"I think so, at least, that's my early assumption. I really don't want to say more until the post-mortem has been carried out. And before you ask, I've arranged for a dear friend of mine to do that as a favour to me. I trust her implicitly. He'll be well cared for under her expert hands."

"No! Why does he have to be cut open?" her mother screeched.

"It's the law, Mum. I should have told you, I'm sorry to upset you further."

Her father patted her hand. "Nonsense. We need to know these things, Sara. We appreciate your experience will come in handy during the investigation. Do you know the person in charge?"

"I know of him. He's got a decent track record. I'll keep an eye on him from afar, however, I won't be able to get too involved, not without risking my career."

Her mother shook her head. "That's so wrong. You should be involved. We need to get to the bottom of why a healthy young man is now…dead."

"And the truth will come out eventually, I promise it will."

"What about Maria, his ex, and the kids, they'll need to be told, won't they?" Lesley suggested.

*Run For Your Life*

"True enough. Mum, have you got a phone number or address for her?"

"I have. It's in my address book. Hand me my bag, love."

Lesley picked up her mother's handbag, propped up against the side of the couch, and handed it to her mother who rummaged around inside and produced a small flowered book. She opened it to the correct page and held it out for Sara to collect.

Sara passed it to Carla to jot down the information.

"Thanks, I've got that now." Carla handed it back to Sara's mother.

"I need to go and see her but I don't want to run off. Will you guys be okay?"

"I don't think I'll ever be the same again. It's never good losing a child of that age, is it?" her mother said, ending her sentence by blowing her nose on a tissue that she always kept tucked up her sleeve.

"I know that, Mum." Sara stood, kissed her three relatives and motioned for Carla to join her. "Okay, I'll drop in on my way home. I'm sorry the news couldn't have been better."

None of her relatives replied, so she left the house.

In the car, Sara broke down, the emotions she'd fought hard to control finally breaking through the wall she'd erected in order to stay strong for her parents' sake.

"There, there, let it out," Carla said in a soothing tone.

"That was so hard. I'm not sure how I bloody managed to hold it together in there. I bet they think I'm a cold-hearted bitch."

"Don't be so damn hard on yourself. Someone had to be in control in there, although saying that, I thought your parents handled it quite well."

"I expected more drama, I have to admit. Maybe we're all guilty of letting Tim down. I suppose the guilt will set in and cause friction between us before long. I hope I'm wrong about that."

"Who's to say what feelings will come to the fore, and when? I'm sorry you've had to deal with it, Sara. I hope you find the answers to your brother's death soon."

"Me, too." She wiped her eyes on the cuff of her jacket, relieved she hadn't put mascara on that morning. "Okay, let's get the next bit over and done with. I haven't got a damn clue how this is going to go down. Maria has never been the easiest of people to get along with."

"How old are the kids?"

"They must be around six and eight by now. Shame on me for not staying in touch with my own nieces. In my defence, I've never really been one for kids."

"Not even your own flesh and blood?" Carla asked, appearing to be shocked by her admission.

"Don't start on me. I have the excuse that I was grieving at the time, plus I moved areas and started in a new division."

"Okay, I'm willing to cut you some slack in that case. You really don't like kids? Does Mark know that?"

"Erm...I think so. I can't say the subject has really come up before, or, if it has, I can't remember having the conversation. That makes me sound a right bitch, doesn't it?"

"Idiot. Of course it doesn't. Let's not get into the pros and cons of having a family now, it's neither the time nor the place."

Sara nodded and set off. Maria's house was around twenty minutes away, on the edge of Leominster. "I hope she's in. Maybe I should have rung her first. My head is all over the sodding place."

"We'll assess things once we're there. What if she's moved?"

"We'll cross that bridge if we come to it. I can't say I'm excited to see her. She was always a bit distant with us."

"What's her background?"

"Her parents dropped her off at a children's home when she was three, from what I can gather."

"Holy shit! Hard to believe people can be so cruel."

"Yep. You'd be surprised. Did you see that programme on TV the other night? The *Long Lost Family* crew did a special where kids were just dumped in cardboard boxes on the steps of some establishments. Jesus, I went cold while I was watching it. Anything could have happened to those children. A murderer could have come along, a paedo, someone as bad as that." She shuddered.

Carla tutted and punched her thigh. "Why the fuck would people do it? There are so many loving homes out there crying out for a family, and yet you get fuckers willing to dispose of their kids as if they're a bag of dog poo!"

"I get what you're saying, but there's a flip side: we don't know the adults' circumstances, do we?"

"True enough. So, you think she's got a chip on her shoulder, this Maria?"

"Hard to put a finger on it. Maybe she's mellowed over the years since her split from Tim. I guess we'll find out soon enough."

Sara pulled up outside the house she'd only visited a handful of times in the past. "This is the one. I should have remembered where it was. It hasn't changed much, still needs a lick of paint. From what I can remember, she isn't the domesticated type either, so be aware of that when we go in there."

"Do you want me to stay here?"

"No, come in, if you don't mind."

"Gotcha."

Sara locked the car and knocked on the door. There was no front garden, only a small one at the rear from what Sara could recall.

The door sprang open. Maria's eyes narrowed as soon as she saw Sara. "You! What do you want after all these years?"

"Hi, Maria, is it possible for us to come in?"

"No, not until you tell me what this is about." She stood in the hallway, her arms folded across her slim frame, in a determined stance.

"It's about Tim."

"What about the bastard? Are you aware I've taken him back to court for the maintenance he's neglected to pay this year?"

"No, I wasn't aware of that. Please, it would be better if we did this inside."

"And who the hell is she?"

"Sorry, this is my partner, DS Jameson. We won't take up much of your time, I promise."

"If you must." She flung the door open wide and let them pass, then she slammed it shut. "Come into the lounge. Excuse the mess, Bob and I are giving the place a makeover."

"Bob?"

"Yeah, my fiancé, is there a law against me marrying again? He's good with the kids, unlike their father. He cares about what happens to them, whereas Tim couldn't give a fuck, apparently. Otherwise he'd send the money he owes me. The bloody courts are useless. I haven't got the money to keep fighting him, who has? He's in the wrong. They're his kids as well as mine, and yet the burden of responsibility has landed on my doorstep since he walked out on us."

"How long have you known Bob?"

"Over a year, not that it's any concern of yours. Tim knows he's around, that's probably why he stopped the bloody payments, truth be told. He's a waste of frigging space, that brother of yours. Drunken shit."

"When was the last time you saw him?"

She paused to think. "Sasha's birthday. She was having a party in the back garden. He rolled up, kicked off and spoilt it for her. He stank of bloody booze. You know what? I'm glad he's not in their lives now, but he should still pay the damn maintenance he owes. Kids cost money to feed and clothe. Why should Bob do that when they're not even his kids? He's on minimum wage but he loves them as if they were his own. We saved up for months to buy all the stuff needed to decorate this place; it was his priority to make this a proper home for the kids. There's no way we could afford to sell up and buy something else, so this is the next best thing. Anyway, that's you up to date, not that any of your family appear bothered with the kids either."

"What? That's not fair. Mum and Dad have always kept in touch with you, haven't they?"

"Maybe, but they don't put their hands in their pockets, though, do they?"

"They're pensioners, and Dad hasn't been in the best of health the last few years."

"Yeah, well, we've all got our problems, ain't we? You try explaining to the kids why their grandparents can't be bothered with them."

"You're not being reasonable, at all. They'd love to be more involved, if you let them."

"You've got your opinion and I've got mine. What are you doing here, Sara?"

"I think you need to sit down."

"I'm fine standing. Go on, tell me."

Sara inhaled and exhaled a few times. "I'm here to tell you that my brother…"

"Otherwise known as the tight bastard. Yeah, what about him?"

Sara tutted. "All right, Maria, less of the snarky attitude, this is hard enough as it is. I'm only here…well, I'm sorry to have to inform you that Tim was found dead in his flat this morning."

"Stop winding me up, Sara."

"I'm not. It's the truth."

Maria sank into the couch behind her and placed a hand over her heart. "What in God's name? How did he die? Damn, I can't believe what I'm hearing. Shit! What am I going to tell the kids?"

"We don't know yet, not until the post-mortem has confirmed the cause of death. I wanted to stop by and tell you personally. I'm sorry it's come as a shock. I've just come from telling my mum and dad and wanted to tell you ASAP for the children's sake."

"How did your parents take it?"

"Not too bad, I don't think it has sunk in yet. I wasn't aware that Tim had treated you and the girls so badly, you should have reached out."

"And said what? I want a handout? Would you have given me one? Bob has been a blessing in disguise, he worships the kids. Jesus, I'm sorry for shouting my mouth off now. Tim might have been a bloody pain in the arse over the years, but he definitely didn't deserve to die."

"No, he didn't. I have to get back to work now. I just wanted to let you know; the kids will have to be told."

Maria let out a shuddering breath. "I know. I'll wait for the right opportunity. Thanks for telling me in person, Sara, I truly appreciate it."

"Okay. Take care of yourself and the girls. I promise to stay in touch more, if that's all right with you?"

"The kids would love to have their aunt and grandparents around, if you can arrange it."

"I'll leave it a few days and broach the subject with Mum. See you soon."

Sara gave Maria an uncomfortable hug at the doorway on the way out.

"Are you all right?" Carla asked, once they'd settled into the car.

"I think so. Maybe some good will come out of this after all. Not sure how Mum and Dad will react, if I'm honest."

"I'm guessing they'd love to see the grandchildren again. It's not as if the break-up was their fault, right?"

"Totally true. Back to base, that's the personal stuff out of the way now."

"Are you sure you're going to be all right to work? Shouldn't you at least take the day off? Your mind must be in turmoil."

"Surprisingly, it's not at the moment. Maybe that will all change later. I need to focus on work. There's nothing I can do about my brother's situation, therefore, I think it would be better if I carry on as normal. Leave Tim's case for Renshaw to sort out. I'll check in daily with him for an update."

Carla chuckled. "He's gonna love that."

"Tough shit! He'll have to get used to it."

# 3

Hunter's nervous energy mounted now as he followed his next target home. Bowen had left work later than anticipated—probably had a lot of dead bodies to cut up himself. Hunter sniggered at the thought. Bowen headed out of town, towards his home. Hunter was aware of where his next target lived, and he knew exactly where to strike.

Bowen took a left up ahead. Not far now. He would need to get closer behind him, in case he lost him. They had joined the road to the Brecon Beacons. Another few miles and his house would come into view on the right. The road widened at this point for a few hundred metres. He put his foot down on the accelerator and sped past him. Hunter left it a moment or two and then slammed his foot hard on the brake and prepared himself for impact.

It never came. Bowen was obviously a conscientious driver and braked, missing his van by inches. A second later, a furious Bowen had left his car and was standing by Hunter's door.

"Get out, you stupid fucker! What are you trying to do, kill us both?"

Hunter lowered his window. "Hey, what's your problem? There was something in the road, I had to swerve to avoid it."

"I didn't see a damn thing. You must have imagined it."

"I swear I didn't. Sorry, mate. All's good. No damage done, right?"

Bowen held up his thumb and forefinger. "Missed you by that much, you fecking idiot. You shouldn't be on the bloody road. So what if you hit something? It's better to kill an animal than cause a fucking accident. Jesus!" He stormed back to his car.

*Getting your knickers in a twist ain't gonna help you, mate!* He picked up the gun wedged between the driver's seat and the handbrake and shot Bowen in the leg.

Bowen dropped to the tarmac, reeling in agony, holding the back of his thigh.

Hunter left the car. Syringe in hand, he sank it into the bemused man's neck. Bowen instantly fell quiet. Had he overdosed him? He didn't think so, although he hadn't anticipated him zonking out so quickly. He hoisted Bowen onto his feet and slung him over his shoulder. It was an effortless action as Bowen had an athletic frame compared to the first victim.

Hunter opened the back of the van and slung him inside. Then he organised the vehicles. He straightened his van first. He slipped on some gloves, jumped in Bowen's car, pulled it over onto the opposite side of the road and parked it on the grass verge. He whipped the keys out of the ignition, locked the door and threw them into the rough grass, close to the car. *That'll keep the cops on their toes!*

He ran back to his van, thankful the road had remained quiet while everything had taken place. Now all he needed to do was get Bowen back to his shack in the woods and let the games begin. He'd need to tend to his wound first.

A few hours later, he'd knocked up sausage, beans and fried eggs for both of them. He wafted Bowen's plate under his nose to bring him round. He stirred slowly but pulled away from Hunter when he realised where he was and what had happened to him.

"My leg. Did you shoot me?"

"Yep. You were pissing me off. Good shot, eh?"

"Do you have a screw loose or something?"

"Probably, although no one has actually diagnosed that." He laughed and tipped his head back.

Bowen shook his head in disgust, and his lip curled up. "Why? Why fucking take a pot shot at me? Because of the accident? Is this a road rage scenario?"

"Nah! I just wanted you to believe it was about that. Your being here relates to something completely different."

"What? Do I know you?"

*You do, but I've changed a lot since you last saw me.* "Nope. Guess again."

"My head hurts. What did you give me?"

"Just a little concoction to knock you out. Worked a treat, too, didn't it?"

"You're sick! Why are you doing this to me? I need to get home to my family."

"I'm sure Leah and little Isla will be doing just fine without you."

The shock registered on Bowen's face, and he blustered, "What? You know my family's names, how? Who the fuck are you?"

"Ah, so many questions. You know what? Why don't we eat up and then I'll consider whether I tell you or not? I'm bloody starving." Hunter picked up his knife and fork and tucked in, keeping a cautious eye on his captive who was staring blankly at him. Halfway through his meal, he asked, "Something wrong? Is it not to your liking?"

"I can't eat. I feel sick. I need to know what's going on here, why you're holding me."

Hunter pointed his knife at Bowen. "You need to be more grateful."

"I do? For what? You kidnapping me? Holding me here against my will?"

"Do you see any restraints on you? How am I holding you here against your will? You're free to go at any time—if you're willing to pay the consequences, that is."

"What consequences? What the fuck are you talking about? I just want to go home to my wife and child. What's wrong with you?"

"Shut up and eat your ruddy dinner, you ungrateful bastard." He pointed at Bowen again. "I know what, let's think of this as your last meal."

"What's that supposed to mean? Last meal?"

"You heard me. Now shut up. I'm enjoying mine."

They both fell silent, Hunter's gaze never leaving Bowen. He could imagine the cogs in his brain working overtime. Trying to figure out if there was a way out of the predicament he'd found himself in. Bowen looked over at the door.

"Go on, make my day!" Hunter warned.

"What? I'm getting my bearings, that's all. Tell me what this is about. I haven't got the foggiest."

"You will, soon."

Bowen's face contorted with anger. "You bastard. You can't keep me here against my will."

Hunter shrugged. "Go on, you're free to go at any time." His gaze drifted to the hunting rifle he'd placed on the upturned crate.

"You think you can scare me? I ain't scared of you."

Hunter laughed. "You might want to tell your face that. I don't think it's received the internal message, just saying."

Bowen's shoulders sagged. He picked up his plate and sliced through the sausage and egg.

"Good man, it'll be worth it. You'll need to keep your strength up for what I have in store for you later."

Bowen dropped his knife and fork, spat the food out and pushed his plate away. "I'd rather starve, it tastes fucking greasy as hell anyway."

"Tastes just fine to me. Your loss, buster." Hunter continued with his meal, groaning with appreciation.

Bowen buried his head in his hands.

"Something wrong?"

"Are you fucking kidding me? Of course something's wrong, I've been shot. I want to go home to my family. You have no right holding me here like this."

Hunter shrugged and held out his arms. "Like I've already told you, you're free to go, mate, but you'll need to suffer the consequences if

*Run For Your Life*

you step outside that door before I tell you to leave. Have you got that?"

"Yeah, loud and clear. At least tell me why you've kidnapped me."

"You'll find out soon enough. I'm busy eating my grub for now. You're missing out. Stonkingly good it is, too."

"It's vile, dripping in grease. You don't get a physique like this by stuffing trash like that down your neck."

Hunter chortled. "You think I'm fat, is that it?"

"I didn't say that. I treat my body like a temple, only eat good wholesome food."

"Are you telling me you never crave a burger now and again?"

"I didn't say that, I eat burgers that are healthy."

"You talk a load of bollocks, anyone ever tell you that before?"

"No. It's true. Burgers that are made with less fat."

"Shut the fuck up. I'm not going to listen to you trying to justify what you put into your belly. Men like you make me wanna puke. Been listening to that wife of yours, no doubt."

"Wrong! I have a fitness guru who goes through this stuff with me, if you must know."

"Jesus! I've never heard such drivel. Enough shit has come out of your mouth, now shut the fuck up. Let me eat my grub in peace."

"Hey, man, you're welcome to that tripe."

Hunter's patience declined. He threw the knife at Bowen, missing the side of his face by inches.

"What the…?"

"Yeah, I missed on purpose. Don't worry, my aim will be better tomorrow," he told him, snatching the knife off Bowen's plate.

"What are your intentions?"

"You'll find out tomorrow."

"At least have the decency to tell me what this is about."

"Why? There's nothing you can either say or do that will change the outcome, so what does it matter?"

"You're warped, you must be."

"It's been said many times." Hunter finished his meal and took the two plates over to the sink. He angled himself so he could see if Bowen moved towards him as he rinsed the plates. They weren't perfect, but they would do.

Bowen never moved a muscle, although his gaze drifted around the room and rested on the front door. Hunter had a feeling that once he was asleep, Bowen would make his move. He'd be on his guard later, anticipating his escape.

He left the dishes draining and returned to the armchair by the fire that was now spitting its way through the large chunk of wood he'd thrown on it to take the chill off the cabin when they'd arrived. "Ah, that's better. Warm enough, are you?"

"I'm fine. Come on, tell me what this is about."

"I know, let's play a game first. You tell me what's gone on in your life and then I'll reveal all."

"Meaning what?"

"Are you thick? Tell me about all the major events that have taken place in your past. Go!"

"Umm...I left school at eighteen, with a few exams under my belt. Is that the type of thing you want to know?"

"Yep, go on. You've got me intrigued now, sitting on the edge of my seat in anticipation," he replied, his response dripping with as much sarcasm as he could muster.

"Bollocks. I ain't saying anything else."

Hunter picked up the gun and waved it at him. "I told you to continue."

"Why? What's the point? You've obviously got an agenda."

"True. The point is, I want to know if you'll admit to what you did."

Bowen's eyes narrowed and then widened as if something had dawned on him.

"Go on, do tell. I'm dying to hear what you're thinking right now."

"I'm not thinking anything."

"Liar. Don't piss me off. The more you tick me off the worse your punishment is going to be, you hear me?"

"Yeah, I hear you. This is about Emma, isn't it?"

Hunter laid his gun across his lap and applauded. "Bingo. See, you're not as dumb as you look."

"Why? After all this time?"

"These things take a lot to organise. I've been following you lot around for years, biding my time, waiting for the right opportunity to present itself. The time is right. Retribution is the name of the game now. You should have eaten the food, it's going to be your last meal on this earth, shithead. Tomorrow the fun begins."

"What the hell are you talking about, are you saying you're going to kill me?"

"Yep. Not until I've had some fun with you, though. You'll see at dawn. Ever seen that time of day before, have you?"

"Of course I have. But why? Why now? What about my family? They need me."

"They need you? Does your wife know? What you did in the past?"

Bowen's chin dipped to rest on his chest, and his shoulders sank. "No. It's something I chose not to tell her."

"Why?"

Scratching the side of his head, Bowen admitted, "Because the shame would've been too much for me to handle."

"Too much for *you* to handle?" Hunter demanded, incensed.

"I didn't mean it in that respect. Shit! You're making me screw up my words."

"I am? Clear your thoughts. Ignore your wife and child, for now. Tell me why you did it. What was going through your head at the time?"

"I can't. I've blocked the incident out of my life. We all have."

"Have you? You're telling me you never discuss it as a group?"

"That's right. We made a pact never to speak about it. We all regret it, I swear we do."

"Is that right? Why is that?"

Bowen shrugged. "I don't know. Well, yes, I do, it was a genuine mistake that we regret happening."

"A genuine mistake, eh? A genuine mistake is cutting someone up on the motorway when your turning is coming up. A genuine mistake is taking someone's drink off the bar, thinking it's your own. You get where I'm going with this?"

"Yes. I'm sorry. Look, that all happened years ago. Time has elapsed. We've all got on with our lives, even Emma."

He lashed out and punched Bowen in the face. "Don't say her name. You're not worthy. It sounds disgusting when you say it."

"Ouch! What the hell? Jesus, I sense I'm damned if I do and damned if I don't. You want me to talk about it, but when it comes to the crunch you don't want to hear the truth."

Hunter glared at him. "You're scum, you all are. Your days are numbered. I'll exact revenge on Emma's behalf. How could you have done that to her?"

"I don't know. We were young and impetuous, we didn't know any better back then, I promise. We regret our actions, we all do."

"Enough for you to want to apologise to Emma?"

Bowen stretched out his neck and waggled it from side to side. "If I had the chance, I would tell her how sorry I was. I never got that chance."

"You think it would matter a jot to her? After what you did, you think a few *insincere* words would do the trick in putting things right?"

The slant in Bowen's shoulders gave him the answer he needed.

"I'm done with you. Shut up and go to sleep." He picked up his gun and moved towards his bed, placing the weapon close to his side. "And don't go getting any ideas. I'll have this beauty close to hand to quell any desires you might have of escaping. Here's yet another warning for you: I'm a light sleeper."

"I won't, I promise. Where am I supposed to sleep?"

"On the couch. Don't insult me by telling me it's not good enough. It's either that or I chain you up outside like a dog. The choice is yours, arsehole."

"I'm fine where I am. Thank you," Bowen mumbled.

"For what? You can thank me in the morning, when it's all over. You'll actually be begging me to put you out of your misery by the time I've finished with you, I can guarantee it."

*Run For Your Life*

"What? I don't understand why you're intent on doing this, punishing me."

"I'm bored now, go to sleep." Hunter's eyelids drooped. He'd had an intense, somewhat adrenaline-filled day. Fairly confident Bowen wouldn't attempt to escape, he drifted off to sleep.

Hunter woke up to the dawn chorus and stretched, almost forgetting where he was for a moment or two, until his mind registered that his gun was poking in his side. "Morning. Sleep well, did you?"

"No. I've barely slept all night. The couch is lacking the padding to give someone a comfortable night's sleep."

"Ungrateful shit. Coffee?"

"Thanks, that would be good. I need to use the loo."

"In there. The window is locked, don't try to get out. I'll know if you attempt it."

"I won't, you have my word."

"Ha! Very well. On you go." Hunter busied himself making them both a drink but kept one ear trained on the bathroom in the corner until Bowen came back into the room. "We don't have time for breakfast. I'm not your servant. I gave you the option of eating last night, but you threw it back in my face. We'll drink this and get cracking."

"Doing what? What have you got planned for me?" Bowen's voice squeaked with the strain.

Hunter turned on the spot and grinned. "You'll see, all in good time."

# 4

Sara had got used to her sad loss. Her brother's untimely death had now been dealt with internally. It had been forty-eight hours since she'd found him lying in his flat. She arrived at work with a lighter heart than when she'd left a couple of days before. She'd taken the previous day off at the insistence of DCI Price. Carla had also encouraged her to take time off. Mark couldn't wangle the full day, however, he'd managed to get the afternoon off after juggling some of his minor appointments around.

She smiled, remembered the afternoon they'd spent together, walking down at the nature reserve by the River Lugg. Peace and tranquillity had been the order of the day for both of them. Sara hadn't really told Mark much about Tim. She'd spent the afternoon regaling him with funny stories about their childhood. Which had upset her more than she'd bargained for, all the angst and anger of recent years dissipating to be replaced by laughter and love, leading her to wonder where their once close relationship had gone.

Her mother had rung every few hours the previous evening, unable to believe her son was dead. Guilt edged her voice. Sara tried to reassure her, to tell her mother it wasn't her fault, but she'd refused to listen.

Now, with most of the funeral arrangements made during her day off, she could get back to solving the ongoing investigation. She breezed through the reception area, and Jeff seemed surprised to see her.

"I'm fine, don't worry about me," she said, not giving him the chance to speak.

"You look pale, are you sure?"

"Honestly, I wouldn't be here if I didn't feel up to it. Any news for me?"

"I'll let Carla fill you in on that, she's already up there."

"Good to know. See you later."

"Aye, you will that."

Jeff buzzed the door open for her to enter. She climbed the stairs, acknowledging a few uniformed officers on their way down.

The team were all hard at it when she walked into the room. "Morning, guys. Where are we at?"

"I wasn't expecting you back so soon," Carla said, doing a double-take.

"Oh, ye of little faith. I told you I'd only need a day to recover from the shock. Anything new, or did you avoid answering my question on purpose?"

Carla rolled her eyes. "No, I didn't. I was more concerned about your well-being."

"By that you mean my mental state, correct?"

Carla sighed and glanced down at the paperwork she was dealing with. "Whatever. Think what you like."

Sara cringed, not liking the sound of her partner's tone. She moved closer to her desk. "Hey, there's no need to be so touchy, I was only pulling your leg."

"Sorry. It's the pressure, I suppose. You know how much I hate being in charge in your absence."

"Well, I can't understand why, you've always coped admirably in the past. What's up?"

"Missing Persons rang this morning, they think they've got a match for our victim."

"That's great news. Why the horse-like face?"

Carla looked puzzled.

"Not a good joke if I have to explain myself. Why the long face?" Sara waved her hand. "Forget it."

"Because not ten minutes ago we received a call about yet another victim."

"What? Are they linked?"

"Possibly. I'll let you be the judge of that."

It was Sara's turn to frown.

"We've been summoned to join Lorraine at the scene," Carla said.

"Okay. And are you going to share with me where that is?"

"Keyhole forest."

Sara groaned. "Don't tell me. Another victim who was an intended target."

"Seems that way. Want to set off now?"

"We'll take a coffee with us. You know what I'm like without my normal quota of caffeine running through my veins."

"Thought you might say that. I won't say no, if you're buying."

"Anyone else?" Sara shouted.

The rest of the team all called out their orders, and she bought the drinks.

"Okay, we're out of here." Sara handed the drinks around and ignored her office and what lay awaiting her in the form of the daily post.

Lorraine crouched, observing the body in the densest part of the forest. "Nice of you to join me, *eventually*."

"Give me a break, I'm grieving. That's my excuse and I'm sticking to it," Sara replied.

"Ouch! I suppose I asked for that. How are you?"

"Numb but managing to hold it together, unlike my mother. Let's stick to business, shall we? I'm fed up of being maudlin. What have we got?"

Lorraine gestured towards the victim. "Young man by the name of

Wesley Bowen. There's a photo in his wallet of him with a woman and a young child."

"Shit! A family man, not so good. Same MO, I take it?"

"Yep, the similarities are startling."

"Startling? In what respect."

"I won't know for certain until I get him back to the mortuary but I suspect the wounds are similar, as in, he was shot in the same places as victim one. Hard to discount the facts."

"Crap, was he killed here or just dumped here?"

"I think, as with victim one, he was hunted down, tracked through the woods, and then killed here. There are signs of him racing through the trees, judging by the wispy lashes on his cheeks."

"Anything else?"

"Not really. I'll be able to fill you in more once I've carried out the PM. His ID and wallet are in the evidence bag, you're welcome to have a look." Lorraine pointed a chubby finger at the bag a few feet away from the victim's head.

Already suited in protective clothing, Sara picked up the ID with her gloved hand and studied it. "Carla, take down this address." She waited for Carla to withdraw her notebook from inside her coveralls. "Sixty-five Oakland Drive. Bridge Sollers. Do you know it?"

"I do," Lorraine chipped in. "It's out on the Brecon Road, the A438."

"Ah, okay, I've not ventured out that way much since moving here, and yet, I admire the view from that direction every morning from my office."

"Nice area, sparsely populated from what I can remember. Do you know much about the area, Carla?"

Carla shook her head. "Not really, I can't add anything else."

"Okay then. We'll hang around here for a little while, have a nosey, and then call in to see his wife or partner. Carla also mentioned that we've got a name for the first victim as well. We'll need to visit the next of kin on that one while we're out, too."

"Busy day ahead of you, or are you just saying that to avoid me dishing out another invitation to attend a second PM?"

"Not intentional, and the thought never crossed my mind. I guess we'll leave you to deal with that, love."

Lorraine poked her tongue out. "Spoilsport. I love seeing you coppers squirm."

"You mean you get off on it."

Lorraine chortled and got back to appraising the victim with her team.

Sara motioned for Carla to join her, and together they plodded through the undergrowth. "Is this place far denser than the last, or is that my imagination?"

"It seems it. Creepy as hell. Can you imagine the bloody fear running through the two victims, knowing that someone was tracking them and taking shots at them?"

"I agree. I wonder if he's picking random vics or whether there's a connection between the two men."

"There's no telling yet, not until we've spoken to the next of kin. Either way, I can't get it out of my head how terrified these men would have been before they took their last breath."

"True enough. Let's keep our eyes open for further clues."

They scoured the area but found nothing. Aware they had several priority visits to make, Sara decided they should leave the crime scene to Lorraine and her team and get back to their own hectic schedule.

Sara slapped the pathologist on the back and made her jump. "We'll be off if you have nothing else for us, Lorraine."

"Jesus Christ, you scared the shit out of me."

"Sorry. We'll be in touch soon."

"If not sooner. Be good."

After trekking through the trees to find the car again, they disrobed, placed the suits in evidence bags and handed them to a uniformed copper to deal with.

While Sara drove, Carla sorted out the address for the first victim which they planned to visit after breaking the news to Wesley Bowen's wife.

"Looks like a fun-filled day ahead of us. Just what I need to keep my mind off my own problems," Sara stated.

"Yeah, it's going to be emotionally draining, I'll give you that."

They exited the car and approached the terraced cottage squashed in the centre of a row of five identical houses. Sara inhaled then exhaled a breath before a woman in her mid-twenties answered the door. Red eyes and a sore nose gave Sara the impression that the woman had been crying non-stop for hours.

"Leah Bowen, can we come in?"

"Are you the police?"

"Sorry, yes, DI Sara Ramsey, and my partner, DS Carla Jameson."

She led them into the lounge. "Okay, if it's bad news I'll have to take Isla upstairs. She's my daughter."

"I think that would be a good idea. Would you like to ring someone, get them to come and be with you?"

"Maybe that would be best. I'll ring my mum."

"We'll watch Isla while you make the call."

"Thank you. I won't be a second." Leah snatched her phone off the small table and rushed into the hall. "Mum, can you come over? The police are here, I think it's bad news. I need you to look after Isla for me."

Sara smiled when Leah re-entered the room.

"Mum's on her way, she's only two minutes up the road. Please don't say anything yet, I'm not sure I could cope." Tears were already forming in her eyes, and as Leah bent to pick up her adorable daughter, one slipped onto her cheek.

The child zeroed in on it and wiped it away. "Mummy, you cwying, why?"

"I'm all right, darling. I have something in my eye. Guess what, Nanna will be here soon."

"Yay, Nanna!"

Sara's heartstrings jerked, and her own eyes puddled with tears at the touching scene. She turned her back and wiped her eyes on the sleeve of her jacket. Carla raised an eyebrow to check if she was okay, and she nodded, reassuring her partner that all was good, for now.

Within a few minutes, a slim woman with a flushed complexion barged into the room. "Hello, what news do you have?"

"Mum, take Isla into the kitchen, will you? I need to speak to the officers alone."

"Oh my, yes, of course." She reached out for Isla and paused to hold her daughter's gaze for a second or two. "I love you."

Leah nodded. "Don't make me worse. I love you, too. We won't be long."

Grandmother and child left the room. Leah sucked in a breath and invited Sara and Carla to take a seat. They sat opposite her.

Sara placed her forearms on her thighs and sat on the edge of the chair. "It is with regret we're here to tell you that Wesley's body was found early this morning." She suddenly realised she hadn't bothered asking Lorraine who had discovered the body. She gave herself an imaginary dig in the shins for slacking in her role.

Leah stared at her, her head gaining momentum as it shook. "No, this can't be true. How? Why?"

"We're awaiting the results from the post-mortem. He was found in Keyhole Forest, do you know that area?"

"No. I've heard of it, I think, but I can't say we've ever visited it as a family. What was he doing there?"

Sara chose her words carefully. "We believe your husband was probably chased by someone."

"Chased? What does that mean?"

"Perhaps you can give us a bit of background information on your husband."

"Such as what? He was hard-working, loved being with me and Isla. We had a good life. God, and now you're telling me that someone did this on purpose? It wasn't an accident?"

"We believe so, yes. When did you last see your husband?"

"Two days ago. In the morning, Isla and I cooked him breakfast before he set off for work."

"And what did he do for a living?"

"He was a butcher in the heart of the city, in the indoor market."

*Run For Your Life*

"Ah yes, I know the one. Did you have any contact with him during the day?"

"No, not at all. I'm usually too busy keeping the little one amused to ring him. I've been going frantic. I lodged a missing person call the night he went missing. They told me they couldn't do anything for twenty-four hours. So I rang back last night, and they noted down the information."

"That's correct. Did your husband travel by car to work?"

"Yes, when I went out searching for him, I used Mum's car to go out there and look for him, I found ours up the road, but it was locked and the keys were missing."

"Up the road? How far?"

"A couple of miles. It's so unusual for him. I tried to ring him, but his phone wasn't connected. I didn't know what had happened. I rang the police immediately, but they weren't prepared to do anything, refused to send a car out to take a look. I've been living on my nerves ever since. Haven't slept a bloody wink in a couple of days and…" She broke down then, sobbed her heart out.

Sara left her seat, perched on the arm of Leah's chair and flung an arm around her shoulders to comfort her. "There, there, it must've been terrible for you not knowing. I'm sorry for your loss."

"How…am…how am I going to cope…without him?"

"There's no denying things are going to be tough for you, especially with the little one. Can you stay with your mum for a while? Maybe that will help initially."

"I suppose so. I hate the thought of disrupting Isla's routine. Will she ever remember him? She's only two. I'm dreading having the conversation with her."

"My advice would be to wait until she's older. I'm no expert, but will a two-year-old be able to comprehend what's going on?"

Leah sniffled. "I suppose you're right. Oh God, I love that man, and now…I can't believe he's gone. How did he get to the forest if his car was here? It's on the other side of town, for God's sake."

"We've yet to figure that out. Maybe someone stopped off and gave him a lift."

"Why would they do that? He was minutes away from home. If the car broke down, he would have rung me."

"Okay, then it sounds like something more sinister has happened. Has your husband mentioned that he'd fallen out with someone recently?"

"No, nothing like that. He got on with everyone. He wasn't the type to bear a grudge. What are you getting at?"

"Maybe someone abducted him."

"For what reason?" Leah sniffed again and then plucked a tissue from the box next to her.

"We don't know. Something isn't adding up. Like you say, if his car broke down then surely he would have rung you."

"He would have, definitely. What if someone offered him a lift home? Maybe he hitched a ride. Oh God. The thought of someone abducting him. I need to know…how did he die?"

Sara swallowed down the lump burning in her throat. "We believe someone tracked him."

"Tracked him?"

"Hunted him in the forest. I'm so sorry, I really didn't want to tell you that."

"It's okay, I pleaded with you to tell me. Jesus, what kind of sick individual would do such a thing?"

"We've yet to find out. I wonder if you've got a spare key to your husband's car."

"I have. It's hanging up in the kitchen." She went to rise from her seat.

Sara stopped her. "No, Carla can get it."

Carla nodded and left the room.

"I can't believe this. He was such a caring man. He adored his daughter, raced home every night to play with her before she went to bed. Not every father would do that after a long day at work."

"I'm sure. Have you seen anyone hanging around the estate lately, a stranger perhaps?"

Leah scratched her head as she thought. "I don't think so, not that I can remember anyway."

Carla came back into the room and held the keys up.

"Okay. We're going to see if we can start the car. Where exactly did you see it?"

"On the grass verge, it's a blue Toyota. Go right at the top of the road, heading back into town, and it's there. You can't miss it."

"We won't be long."

Sara smiled at the young woman whose heart was shattered into tiny pieces. She and Carla jumped back into the car and flew down the road. Sara snapped on a glove and took the keys from Carla. She opened the door and inserted the key into the ignition. The victim's car sparked into life. Her gaze drifted back to where Carla was sitting in her car. She shrugged, at a loss what to bloody think.

Why had Wesley Bowen left his car a few miles from his home? It didn't make sense. The only thought running through her mind was that he must have been abducted. By whom? And why? Just so the kidnapper could kill him?

She secured the car again and circled it, searching for any possible knocks in the car's bodywork. Frustratingly, she didn't find anything.

They returned the keys to Leah. She was eager to hear if they'd found anything. Her hopes were dashed when Sara revealed the truth.

"I'm going to get a SOCO team out here to examine it, just in case. I'll get them to return the car to you once they've finished."

"What's your conclusion?" Leah asked, her chest expanding. She let out the heavy sigh.

"My take is that he was abducted. There's no damage on the car, so we can rule out that he was run off the road, injured and seeking help."

Fresh tears welled up, and Leah asked, "Why? Why would someone want to abduct him? And then go on to ki…" She shook her head, setting the tears free.

"That's the mystery that we will have to figure out. I'm so sorry for your loss. Here's a card, ring me if you need anything. I'll keep you updated as the investigation progresses."

Leah sniffled and took the card. "Thank you. Please, do what you can to find his killer."

"We will."

Sara hurried out of the house and jumped back in the car where Carla had decided to wait for her. "Shitting hell. What the heck is going on here? Why him? He seemed a decent enough family man, according to what his wife said."

"It's still early days. We need to find a possible link between the two men that will give us an indication of what we're looking at here."

"Right, we have two options—no, scrap that, we need to go and see the first victim's next of kin. Have you got the address?"

Carla withdrew her notebook from her pocket and punched the postcode into the satnav while Sara headed back into town.

They were led to a detached property in a quiet cul-de-sac. All the properties appeared to be neatly cared for, built sometime in the thirties. A riot of colour welcomed them onto the cheery close, each garden doing its bit. A July garden, where roses emerged from buds and swayed in the breeze lifting one's spirits, Sara had always thought.

There was a Mini sitting on the gravelled drive in front of the red garage door.

Sara rang the bell. "Here we go again. Remind me why I do this job?"

Carla smiled and whispered, "Because you love it. What else would you do?"

The chain jangled and the door opened. A woman with a pained, concerned expression stood there. "Hello, can I help?"

Sara didn't have the heart to lecture her about safety and the fact she should have left the chain in place before she asked that question. Instead, she produced her ID and introduced herself and her partner.

"Oh no. This is about Doug, isn't it?"

"Maybe it would be better if we came inside." Sara stepped into the house as the woman stumbled backwards against the wall, her foot slipping out of her slippers in her haste to allow them access. "Are you all right?"

"Clumsy me. I'm under the doctor, keep blacking out without a moment's notice. Light-headed most of the time. Let's go into the lounge, I think I need to sit down."

They followed her into the room. Sara pulled back a little and made a face at Carla, suddenly dreading telling the woman of her son's demise.

"Get her to ring a relative now, it's the only way, given her medical history."

Sara nodded. "You're right. Shit! I hate this. Why can't life ever be simple?"

Carla smiled. "Now you know that wouldn't be any fun for us."

"Right!"

Mrs Connor sat in a large leather armchair. She gestured for them to sit on the couch. They sank into the luxuriously soft seats.

Sara cleared her throat. "Mrs Connor, do you have a family member you can call upon to come and sit with you?"

"My sister, but she's at work. Please, call me Barbara. My husband is away at the moment, he's a lorry driver."

"Ah, I see. Barbara, would you mind giving your sister a call? I think someone should be with you at this time."

"I'm only allowed to ring her in extreme circumstances…"

"Please, give her a call."

Trembling took over, and Barbara's body went into meltdown. *Shit! Just what I was trying to avoid.* "Barbara, can you hear me?"

The convulsions erupted and consumed the woman's every limb.

"Bloody hell. I'm going to ring for an ambulance," Carla said without hesitation. She ran into the hallway.

Sara grasped Barbara's hand and squeezed it between hers. "Barbara, where does your sister work? What's her name?"

"Greggs, in town. Jenny Wat…son. Please, he…lp…me."

"Help is on the way. Stay with me, hold my hand, I'm going to ring your sister now." She looked up Greggs' number and rang the shop and asked to speak to the manager.

"Hello." An officious speaking man came on the line.

"Hello, sir, my name is DI Sara Ramsey, and I'd like your permission to speak with Jenny Watson on an urgent matter."

"Can't this wait until she's finished work? She's busy."

"I'm sorry, no, it can't."

He huffed out a breath. "Very well. Hold the line."

Sara nodded and smiled at Barbara. "Hang in there, she's coming now."

"Hello. What do you want?"

Sara introduced herself to the woman and added, "I'm with your sister, Barbara. Is there any chance you can come and be with her?"

"Why? What's wrong with her? Jesus, I'm at work. Unless her life is in danger, I don't think the boss will let me have the time off."

"I don't wish to scare you, but we've just had to call an ambulance. Please, I wouldn't ask if it wasn't an emergency."

"Bloody hell! What's wrong with her?"

"It would be better if you came quickly."

"What if they cart her off to the hospital, should I go there instead?"

"I think it would be better if you came here."

"I'm on my way. Be there soon. Tell her I love her and to remain calm."

"I will. Thanks, Jenny." Sara patted Barbara's hand. "There, she's on her way, whether her boss likes it or not."

Barbara's tremors died down a little. "Oh God, whatever is happening to me? I'm so cold."

Sara spotted a furry throw hanging over the arm of the couch at the other end and raced to get it. She covered Barbara who smiled appreciatively.

"Thank you. What did you want to speak to me about?"

"It can wait. Let's get you sorted first. Do you want a tea or coffee?"

"A tea, hot and sweet would be nice, if you don't mind."

Carla came back into the room to inform them that the ambulance was on its way.

"Can you make Barbara a cup of hot sweet tea, Carla? Thanks."

"Of course."

Barbara sighed, her body nice and still after its sudden spasms. Sara couldn't help but feel relieved that nothing worse had happened to the woman after the turbulent week she'd had so far.

Ten minutes dragged by.

*Run For Your Life*

Sara's ears pricked up at the sound of the ambulance getting closer. "They're here now."

"I feel foolish, you shouldn't have called them, I'm all right now."

"Better to be safe, let them check you over, it can't hurt."

Carla jumped out of her seat to let the paramedics in. She explained what had gone on at the front door and entered the room with a man and a woman in uniform.

"Hello there. She seems a lot calmer now. Her whole body appeared to be trembling out of control. She told us she's prone to having blackouts. I was concerned about that, so we rang nine-nine-nine for assistance."

"Let's see what we've got here then. What's your name, love?" the male paramedic asked.

"Barbara. I feel fine now. I'm so sorry to have wasted your time."

The paramedic smiled. "Nonsense. Let's give you a thorough check over."

Sara backed up, giving him room to assess the woman's vital signs. She took the opportunity to speak to the female paramedic in the hallway. "Sorry for calling you out. We're here to break the news that her son has been murdered. We didn't get that far, though. All I did was show her our IDs and she started convulsing."

"Oh heck! Okay, thanks for warning us. Maybe it would be better to share the news while we're still here, on hand."

Sara puffed out a breath. "Makes sense. I've rung her sister, she should be here soon. Can I tell her then?"

"We're in no rush. Well…within reason, of course."

They both walked back into the room.

The male paramedic laughed with Barbara. He stood. "She's fine, nothing majorly wrong with her anyway. We'll be on our way now then."

"We need to hang around a little while, Bob," his female colleague said.

"Oh?"

The doorbell rang.

"Carla, can you get that for me?" Sara asked.

Carla left and returned with a fraught-looking woman of a similar age to Barbara.

"What on earth have you been up to, you, silly old woman?" She pecked her sister on the cheek and sat on the arm of the chair.

"Sorry to bother you, love. I don't know what's wrong with me. I think they're here about Douglas, and my body couldn't cope. I've been living through hell the last few days, not knowing where he is."

Sara glanced at the female paramedic and chewed on her lip. She crossed the room and knelt on the floor beside Barbara and clutched her hand. "I'm so sorry, Barbara, there's no easy way to tell you this. I'm afraid Douglas won't be coming home again. His body was found a few days ago in the forest."

"What? No, there must be some kind of mistake. He can't be…" Barbara's confused gaze shot between Sara and Jenny.

"Are you sure? One hundred percent sure?" Jenny asked.

"Yes. Barbara reported her son missing. It was that report which led us to formally identify Douglas. I'm sorry for your loss, Barbara. I'm going to need to ask you some questions. Do you think you'll be up to that?"

Barbara seemed understandably shell-shocked by the news. She stared at her sister for guidance. "What do you think? My God, I don't believe he's gone. It can't be true, he's so young."

"I know, love. Let's try and help the officers, maybe they'll be able to catch someone responsible for his death, soon." Tears dripped onto Jenny's cheeks. She was clearly trying to hold it together for her sister's sake even though the news had knocked her own world off its axis.

Barbara nodded. She appeared to be under control and able to continue, so Sara began asking her usual questions.

"When was the last time you saw Douglas?"

"The morning he went missing. I cooked him breakfast, got up at six to do it. He was out of the house by seven. He didn't come home that evening after work; he rang me from the pub, told me he was having a few pints with his workmates. That's the last I heard from him. Oh, Jenny, what am I going to do without him? He was my tower of strength and now he's gone."

"Do you want me to ring Lee? He should come home and be with you."

"He's up north somewhere, he wouldn't appreciate me ringing him." Suddenly, the shock took over, and Barbara's body shook. This time the spasms were far worse than before.

Jenny and Sara were asked to move back by the paramedics, and the man dug in his bag for some form of medication.

"What's that?" Sara asked.

"A sedative. Her body needs to calm down. She'll be fine soon. I'm going to make the call. I think she'd be better off in hospital, they'll be able to monitor her there."

Sara nodded. "Very well. Our questions can wait."

Barbara held out her hand for Sara to take. "Please, that's all I know. Don't let them get away with this."

"I promise you, we'll do everything to prevent that from happening. Try not to worry, be kind to yourself and allow your body to heal, love."

"I will. Maybe Lee should come home after all," Barbara said to her sister.

"Leave it to me. I'll give him a bell now. I won't tell him about Doug, though, not over the phone, it wouldn't be right."

"We're going to leave now. Here's a card." Sara handed it to Jenny. "Ring me if you need anything. We'll try and stay in touch as often as we can. Take care of yourself, Barbara, I think you're doing the right thing going to the hospital. One last thing, if I may? Where did Douglas work?"

"He worked for the council as a road cleaner, not a trendy job by any means, but it brought a regular wage in," Jenny replied before her sister got the chance to say anything.

"Okay. Thanks for that. We'll be off. Take care, Barbara."

"Do your best for us," Barbara said, her voice trailing off as the sedative took hold.

Sara and Carla thanked the paramedics and went back to the car.

"Jesus, I thought she was going to die back there."

Carla closed her eyes for an instant and nodded. "Thank God she didn't. Where to now?"

"I'm feeling fraught, I admit. I think we should go back to the station. I'm going to get Craig and Will to do the legwork for us on this one. I don't think I can face asking the same bloody questions over and over and receiving the same frigging answers all the time. It's driving me nuts."

"I'm with you on that one. There must be a link between these guys. I don't mind starting the digging if you want to take a break."

"A break? Hardly, I have a shitload of paperwork piling up on my desk."

"You're finding it tough, I can tell. You don't need to pretend with me, lady."

"That's because you're perceptive. I know I shouldn't be at work. I'll admit, I'm not at my best right now. Maybe if I hadn't been the one who found Tim, I'd find things a little easier."

"You're right, you shouldn't be at work."

"What else would I do? Dwell on things at home? At least this way it's not on my mind a hundred percent of the time. I'm sorry for being a grouch."

"You haven't been, and even if you were, I'd make allowances for it in the circumstances. You need to learn to start giving yourself a break emotionally, Sara. You're grieving the loss of a close family member. Anyone in your shoes would understand the distress you're going through at this time. Give in to it and stop being so damn hard on yourself. How many balls are you trying to juggle at the moment?"

"Too many. Thanks, Carla. I appreciate what you're saying makes sense."

"Then take heed of my words and give yourself a breather. No one is expecting you to be Superwoman all of the time. Certain things are sent to try us, to push our buttons in this world, and the untimely death of a loved one comes under that umbrella."

"Okay, enough chatting, let's get back to base and let the hard work commence."

## 5

The team listened as Sara brought the whiteboard up to date. Craig and Will volunteered to do the legwork. To be honest, Sara thought they both seemed relieved to be getting out of the office. She sent them off to Wesley Bowen's and Douglas Connor's workplaces. After buying the rest of the team a cup of coffee, setting everyone to work on their specific background checks, instructing them to report any findings directly to Carla for the rest of the day, Sara drifted into her office and closed the door behind her.

She cast a furtive glance at the view, promising herself a day's trekking up the Brecon Beacons once life settled down a little. First there was the rest of the funeral to sort out, and then there were her imminent wedding plans to finalise. She couldn't believe that was only a few weeks away. Tim's death was bound to mar everyone's enthusiasm for their nuptials now. She sensed her wedding was the last thing on her parents' mind at present. *What a bloody mess!*

A few hours into the mind-numbing chore, Carla knocked on her door and poked her head into the room. "Is it safe to come in?"

Sara leaned back and smiled. "Sure, it's not been as painful as I anticipated. What have you got, anything?"

"Something has definitely shown up."

Sara motioned for her partner to take a seat and sat forward again. "Sounds intriguing. What?"

"Well, I set the others working on both men's backgrounds, involving the usual, searching the system to see if they had any record and their financials."

"And?"

"I'm not sure why the names didn't get flagged up before, they should have. Maybe the system was a bit wonky. Anyway, both men have an arrest record."

"For what?"

"Here's where it gets interesting. Back in twenty-fifteen, a gang of five men were arrested for raping a teenage girl; she was eighteen at the time. Here's the thing, the case went to court, but all of them got off."

Sara's mouth dropped open, but she recovered to say, "Shit! How the heck did that happen? No, wait, can you get me the file? I want to see this for myself."

Carla nodded and shot out of the room. She returned carrying a manila folder and handed it across the desk to Sara before she returned to her seat. Sara speed-read the facts of the case, shaking her head continuously. "Jesus, have you read all of this?"

"Yep, it blew my mind. Those guys were nailed to go down for the crime, but the jury let them off."

"Didn't they just? Let me see who was representing them in court." She flipped through a couple of pages and then stabbed her finger at a name that stood out on the page. "Jesus, Barrister John Bridges-Smythe. I've heard of him. He costs big money. Okay, let's not jump to any conclusions here. Using the material in the file, let's see what up-to-date information we can get on the other three men."

"I've got Marissa, Christine and Jill doing just that now. Are you thinking what I'm thinking? This Emma is finally taking her revenge after all this time?"

"Yes, although I'm trying my hardest not to think that. While I understand the need and desire for a woman in her situation to start out on that course, I believe they should resist the temptation. We had a similar case back in Liverpool when I was there." She fell quiet as memories she had successfully pushed to one side resurfaced and set a ball of fire burning in her chest.

"Are you okay?"

Sara ran her tongue over her dry lips. "Fine, I think. Give me a second." Tears surfaced, and her gaze drifted out of the window to the blue sky, decorated with cotton-wool puffs of clouds. *He's up there somewhere, watching over me.* Turning her attention back to Carla, she finished off what she was saying. "Back in Liverpool, the blasted gang, the same one who killed Philip, was accused of gang raping several teenage girls. A few months later, two of the girls teamed up and made a pact to avenge the crimes. They enticed one of the gang members into a house—they'd effectively set up a trap for him." Sara swallowed hard. "What they did to him...well, I know the guy deserved it in one sense, but on the other hand, no one deserved to go like that."

Carla eased forward in her chair. "Wait, you can't stop there. I want all the gory details."

Sara smiled. "I promise you, you don't. For a start, they chopped his dick off."

"Eww...and? No, you're not telling me they forced him to eat it, are you?"

"Glad to see we're finally on the same wavelength. That's exactly what they did. They must have seen that scene from *Game of Thrones* where Ramsay Bolton cut off Theon Greyjoy's penis. Only they took it one step further. The guy ended up choking on it."

"He died? Oh fuck! And what happened to the girls?"

"They were arrested. While awaiting the court trial, the other gang members got hold of them and...well, I don't need to fill in the blanks concerning a gang who lived by the motto of 'an eye for an eye', do I?"

Carla shuddered. "There are some evil, sadistic bastards out there, aren't there?"

"Yep, revenge cases rarely end well, not in my experience. Anyway, let's see what we can find out about...Emma Wyatt, was it?"

She skimmed through the pages to the front of the file and nodded. "Yes, Emma Wyatt. Let's see what shows up there."

Carla stretched her hand out to collect the file.

Sara slammed it shut and gave it to her. "Let me know when the boys are back. They shouldn't be long now."

"Will do." Carla slipped out of the room.

Sara's mind remained in the past, mulling over her husband's murder. That experience had rocked her world, damaged her heart beyond repair, or so she had thought at the time. She was that shocked, although she had never admitted it to her family and friends, she'd contemplated slitting her wrists on more than one occasion. The thought of living without Philip suffocated her. If it hadn't been for Misty, a gift from Philip before his death, she would have done the deed. Instead, she'd uprooted herself and moved to Hereford, to be close to her family. So why hadn't she kept in touch with all of them, namely Tim? Guilt lay heavily on her shoulders, weighing them down.

*I mustn't torture myself. Tim was a lost cause, or was he? Maybe all these months of living in isolation was his cry for help. He was a stubborn man, a proud man even. Jesus, I'm going to miss him, I know that.*

She returned her attention to the last pile of post she had to deal with, ignoring the family's issues for now. It was time to get on with the task at hand, solving these two murders. She reflected on how the investigation had brought painful memories back, even though she'd been successful keeping them buried for years. As much as she hated to admit it, maybe Tim's death was affecting her more than she realised. Something had to change, and quickly, if she was going to remain in charge of the investigation.

Carla summoned Sara about an hour later when Craig and Will arrived back. She hurriedly left the office and stood by the whiteboard, poised with the marker pen in her hand, ready to add any details. Sadly, the boys had very little else for her to add. She'd made the right choice by remaining in the office, at least she'd cleared her desk in their absence.

"Great, sorry you've had a wasted trip, guys. Grab yourselves a drink and we'll go over what the team have discovered since you left us."

Craig headed for the vending machine and returned with a drink for him and Will. He settled into his chair while Sara went over what Carla had found out about the two victims.

"Jesus, are we talking about revenge killings here?" Craig sipped his coffee.

"Let's not make that call just yet. Carla, has anything else come to light about this Emma Wyatt?"

"Here's what we've managed to find between us. She still lives at the family home with her parents and her four-year-old daughter."

Sara gasped. "The daughter, is she a consequence of the rape?"

"That's my assumption," her partner agreed.

"Jesus. Okay, we have to put ourselves in her shoes in that case, living with a child who was conceived through a violent act and who could be the spitting image of her father. I know living with something as harrowing as that would do damage to my head. Ladies, what about you?"

All four female officers in the room nodded.

"It has to," Carla added. "Okay, if that's the case, then why now? Five years after the crime was committed?"

"That's something we're going to have to try and get out of Emma."

"What? We're just going to go storming in there and ask her point blank if she's behind these murders?"

"Yes, that's right," Sara said, then she tutted and wagged a finger at Carla. "Credit me with some sense. As if I'd do something as ludicrous as that."

"Sorry, me shooting my mouth off again. Ignore me."

Sara smiled. "If you insist. So, here's what I suggest. We aim to track down the rest of the gang members; we'll need to make them aware of the situation—"

"What? That we believe Emma is going around bumping off those who raped her?" Carla interrupted.

"No, not in so many words, obviously. We'll make them aware of the two murders and see if they've either been contacted by an outsider or by the other members of the gang recently and go from there."

"Ah, I see, yes, I'm with you now. I told you to ignore me."

Sara grinned at her partner. "Consider it done now. The dilemma is whether we do this tonight or leave it until tomorrow."

Both Craig and Carla raised their hands to speak.

Sara deliberately pointed at the young constable. "As Carla instructed me to ignore her, go ahead, Craig."

"I would definitely opt for this evening, boss. Bearing in mind the victims have both gone missing after work—that is, if we're not too late."

Sara followed his gaze. The clock on the wall showed five-forty-five. "Okay, let's work quickly, peeps. Find out where these guys work, pronto!"

Sara's gut tied itself into knots. Was she guilty of delaying the inevitable? Should she have been more on the ball in the first place and asked the other team members to have sourced the information ASAP? Or was she just being too damn hard on herself because of the state her mind was in? Either way, she hated the fact that she was doubting her police skills. That had never happened in her fifteen-plus years on the force, so why now?

# 6

Hunter arrived at the Greyhound pub near the racecourse. It was quiet except for a few cars dotted here and there. He wondered if he was too late to catch his target. He let out a relieved sigh when he realised that none of the cars belonged to James Stanley, the third name on his list.

He tucked his van behind the rubbish skips and got out of the vehicle. Dressed all in black with a balaclava itching his face, he waited, ready to pounce.

Stanley's car pulled into a space close to the door. Hunter bided his time, aware there were CCTV cameras angled at the entrance. There would be no getting away from them, not unless he damaged them in some way. He'd have to see if he had time to do that before leaving the scene. He prepared himself, annoyed Stanley was taking forever to leave his vehicle. Finally, the driver's car was kicked open by Stanley. He was distracted, playing with his mobile. Hunter swooped in, grateful Stanley wouldn't hear him coming.

Hunter was two steps behind him before Stanley appeared to sense him close by. He turned and gasped. "What the fuck? Who are—"

The spray from the can silenced Stanley, most of it entering his mouth as he ranted.

"Don't fight it, shithead." Hunter injected his neck with the clear liquid.

The guy fought, his arms and legs striking out, but it proved pointless as the sedative worked its magic. Hunter dragged his captive to his van and opened the back door. He shoved the inert body in, safe in the knowledge that Stanley was genuinely unconscious and not just pretending, and returned to the front of the pub. He carried a metal bar. The cameras were within easy reach. He smashed them, one by one—there were three of them—and then he ran back to the van and put his foot down, leaving the car park before anyone else could arrive.

He tapped his hands on the steering wheel to the upbeat tempo coming from the radio and drove out to the lodge in the woods. Fifteen minutes later, Stanley was sitting on his couch, where the other two bastards had sat over the last few days before him. This time Hunter had something new in store for Stanley. He'd been singled out for special treatment for a specific reason.

Filling the kettle and a mug with water, Hunter returned to Stanley and threw the contents of the mug in his face.

Stanley shook his head, the water rousing him from his deep sleep. "What the…? Who are you? What the fuck is going on here?" He glanced at his hands, tied behind his back.

Hunter had decided Stanley was more likely to be trouble than the other two lads so had taken the precaution of securing his hands and legs.

A dog barked outside the cabin.

"Was that a dog? Help, please, someone help me. There's a crazy guy in here, he's holding me against my will. Help me, please!"

Hunter shook his head and grinned. "The dog belongs to me, you fecking moron. Save your voice. No one is within earshot to rescue you."

"Why are you doing this? What have I ever done to you? I don't even know you."

"You know of me, I can assure you." Hunter pointed at him. "Actually, we have met, a few years back, after…" He intentionally let his sentence trail off. It was part of his torture technique for this one.

"I don't. I'm good with faces. Do you come in the pub? Are you angry at me for something I've done or haven't done at work? Come on, give me a clue. Let me try and put things right. I could give you free drinks for a month or something to make up for any mistakes I've made in the past. Give me a break, mate, come on."

Hunter took a step towards him, drew his arm back and punched Stanley in the face. "Shut the fuck up, you mindless jerk. You seriously think this is about you watering down one of my drinks or short-changing me at some time? You're even denser than I took you for."

"Tell me then. What am I supposed to have done wrong?"

"Coffee? This is a one-time offer. Either accept it or go without until the morning."

"Morning? You intend keeping me here all night? Why? What the fuck have I ever done to you?"

"I'm bored now, stop asking dumb questions. I'll give you a chance to think about what you've done wrong in your life and see if you can discover the answer for yourself."

Hunter went over to the sink and filled two cups with coffee. "Sugar?"

"Yes, one."

"A thanks wouldn't go amiss."

"Sorry, thanks. What do you mean, think about my past?"

"Just that. You need to take a good look at yourself. Reflect what you've done in your life and see what pops up. My guess is that it won't take you long to figure it out, not unless you've committed numerous crimes over the years. Have you?"

"No. My record is clean."

Hunter finished making the drinks and returned to the couch. He placed the two mugs on the upturned crate in front of Stanley.

"How am I supposed to drink that with my hands tied?"

"I'll give it to you when it's cooled down. We were talking about your record. Go on, I'm intrigued to know why you believe you have a clean one."

James Stanley dipped his head and sighed. "All right, all right, so I lied."

"Not a good start. Make sure you don't do it again, or the consequences will be a darn sight more severe, just warning you. Don't take me for a fucking amateur, boy."

"I won't, I promise. Please, if this is anything to do with the misdemeanour I did back in my teens, I regret it."

"How much?"

"What?"

"How much do you regret it? Has it blighted your life? Has it made you reconsider how you treat people? Women in particular? Come on, tell me, I'm interested to know what's going on in that head of yours."

"Why? What are your intentions?"

"Ah, wouldn't you like to know?"

"Yes, otherwise I wouldn't have asked," Stanley snapped back.

Hunter kicked him in the leg. "Less of the wisearse cracks, mate. You've done your chances of survival a lot of harm there."

"Sorry, please, don't hold it against me."

"What are you talking about? The crime, or the fact your mouth ran away from you?"

"Both. I've regretted my actions back then, it's remained with me all these years. I was in the wrong, I know that now. Mistakes happen when we're kids, right? We do things out of necessity at times, you understand that, don't you?"

"Out of necessity? What possessed a brat of your age back then to contemplate raping an innocent girl?"

Stanley tipped his head back and then let it drop forward again. "I'm sorry. We all were. But the court found us innocent. That was the end of it. Justice was served."

"Listen to your fucking self, will you? Justice was served? For who? Not for her."

"She's got on with her life, just like the rest of us. No harm done in the end."

Burning anger flared and roared through Hunter's veins. He pummelled the insensitive bastard with his fists until he lay unconscious on the couch. Then he stared down at the vile individual and spat on him until his saliva dried up. "Fucking moron. If only you knew."

7

They raced into the Greyhound pub after the manager had rung the station.

Sara showed him her ID and introduced herself and Carla. "Can you tell me what happened?"

He was pacing behind the bar, snapping at any member of staff who got under his feet. "Sodding hell, Helen, I said make yourself useful elsewhere. Work on your initiative for a change and go wipe down some menus or something. Just get out of my sodding way."

"Mr Lawson, can you calm down and tell us what happened?"

"Someone fuc...damaged my security cameras, that's what! Five grands' worth of equipment. The bloody things were all right when I opened up at lunchtime. I swear, if I catch the mindless bastards who did this, their lives won't be worth living. Trade is bad enough as it is without having to fork out for replacement equipment." He clutched a section of hair and yanked on it. "Livid I am, in case you hadn't noticed. Working here, putting in eighteen-hour days most of the time, and people come along and wipe out my profit for the goddamn week. Why do I frigging bother?"

"I'm sorry to hear that. When you called the station, you mentioned one of your staff had gone missing, a James Stanley, is that right?"

"Yep. He showed up because his car is out in the front. I've tried ringing him, and his phone rang three times then went dead. He's not the type to let me down. He loves working here and gets on great with the punters."

"That was going to be my next question, whether he'd fallen out with a punter recently."

"Nope, like I said, he's a likeable lad. I tried ringing his missus, and she told me he left for work in plenty of time. Now I've got her all worked up, and she's bloody about to drop any minute."

"Drop? As in, give birth?"

"That's right. Poor girl was stressed out."

"We'll need to go and see her, can you give us her address?"

"I thought you might want that, so I've wrote it, or should that be *written* it, down for you?"

Sara smiled. "Written. Thanks, that's much appreciated."

He handed Sara the scrap of paper.

"Your CCTV footage, maybe you can have a look at it for us."

"Shit. Come through, it might show me who the bloody culprit is. Good thinking."

Sara and Carla walked around the bar and followed him into the back office.

"I have my uses," Sara murmured.

"Right. Take a seat if you can find one. The place is a mess, sorry, not enough hours in the day, and I've got to sleep when I can. Sorry again, you don't want to hear me whinging about the hours I put in. Part and parcel of the job, right? Let's see what we've got here."

After a bit of tinkering, the screen sprang into life. He whizzed through the lunchtime rush and the customers arriving during the afternoon, and then, as the clock sped around to five o'clock, a young man arrived and got out of his car. At that moment, they watched another man dressed in black approach him, attack him and drag him back to a van. Then the attacker damaged the cameras with an iron bar.

"Damn, he's wearing a bloody mask!" Sara noted.

"Not helpful. What about his vehicle? Can you rewind to when he pulled into the car park?" Carla suggested.

Lawson did just that. "Here." He froze it and moved the image a few seconds at a time. "No plate on the van. That figures."

"Shit!" Sara muttered, smacking her fist against her thigh. "I hate a canny criminal. Okay, if you can give us a copy showing the incident, Mr Lawson, that would be a great help."

"I'll do that for you now. It won't take me a jiffy."

Sara turned away to speak to Carla. "Seems to me like we're dealing with a professional here."

"Well, if it's who we think it is, they've had five years to think up a decent plan of action."

"What? Did I hear right? You know who the person responsible is?" Lawson asked, mystified by the look of things.

"Something came to light today, it's just an inkling at this point. We can't say any more, I'm sorry."

"Well, it's nice to know you've got a lead. What now? Why would this person want to abduct James? That's what's blowing my mind."

"We're unsure about that. Is it ready?" Sara pointed at the machinery, eager to get on the road again.

He tapped a few keys, and a disc popped out of the machine. "There you go. I hope you find it useful."

"I'm sure we will. Thanks for your help."

Sara and Carla raced out of the pub and into the car.

"So what do we do now? Yet another person has been abducted. Shouldn't we go and see this Emma Wyatt?" Carla asked.

"That's the dilemma. On the one hand I think we should pay Stanley's girlfriend a visit, make her aware of the situation, but on the other, you're right, we should be going to Emma's. How are you fixed for time?"

Carla shook her head. "That's the least of our problems. Choose which one we visit first."

Sara gunned the vehicle into life.

"The girlfriend. I'm conscious of the fact she's heavily pregnant and probably worried out of her mind. I need to make sure she's okay first, get a family member to sit with her. I'm also aware that I could be screwing up big time here. Half an hour tops, I promise. Her place isn't far from here."

"I agree. Time isn't on our side, though, Sara."

"I know." She switched the siren on and shot off.

James Stanley's house was in the middle of a large estate of similar-looking houses. Sara exhaled a large breath and exited the vehicle and, with Carla right behind her, she marched up the cracked concrete path and rang the bell. An older woman, perhaps in her late fifties answered seconds later.

Sara and Carla held up their IDs.

"DI Ramsey and DS Jameson. Is James Stanley's girlfriend at home?" Sara kicked herself for not getting the girlfriend's name off the pub manager.

"She is. Oh God, is this about James? The manager rang Sienna, concerned, and she rang me. I came straight away. I'm her mother. Come in, please. Do you have some news for us?"

"Thank you. Not as such. We're aware of the situation."

"Which is? I wish someone would tell us what the hell is going on." The woman's voice rose as she spoke.

Sara laid a hand on her arm. "Please, try and remain calm. What's your name?"

"It's Josie. I'm trying to remain calm. It's difficult when your daughter is eight and a half months pregnant, though. I'm worried about what effect this is going to have on the baby. She's had a rough pregnancy, one way or another, thanks to that idiot." Her gaze dropped to the floor as if she regretted her words as soon as they'd tumbled out of her mouth.

"Would you care to enlighten us about that?"

"Not really. He's got a temper on him where women are concerned, that's all I'm prepared to say on the subject."

"Mum! What are you saying?" a heavily pregnant woman screeched from the doorway.

"I'm sorry, love, you weren't supposed to hear that. You know how I feel about him. He should look after you and the bairn, not beat you black and blue."

"Jesus Christ!" her daughter objected.

The girl, who Sara presumed was Sienna, marched back into the room. Sobs soon filled the hallway, both from the mother and Sienna.

*Bugger, just what I need to deal with right now. This is going to be an emotional mess. Wrong call, Sara girl, you should have gone to Emma's instead.*

"Let's go through and try and calm things down a bit, eh?" Sara rubbed the older woman's arm and nudged her towards the doorway to what she thought would be the lounge. Once Josie moved, Sara rolled her eyes at Carla as if to say 'here we frigging go'.

Mother and daughter kept to opposite sides of the room. Josie leaned against the ledge of the bay window while Sienna sat on the couch with her head buried in her hands. Sara sat close to Sienna. Carla remained by the door.

"Sienna. We've just come from the Greyhound pub. I have some bad news that you need to hear."

She dropped her hands and stared at Sara. "What? Is James all right?"

"We don't know is the honest answer. He turned up for work at the usual time, but before he could enter the building someone attacked him, knocked him out and, well…we believe he's been abducted."

"What are you telling me? That someone has kidnapped him? Why?" Her voice rose several levels.

"We're not sure about that at this time. I don't want to cause you any more unnecessary upset but I need to ask you some questions, if that's okay?"

"Of course, but what would I know? About this, I mean. I know nothing. I can't believe this." She glanced down and smoothed a protective hand over her bump.

"We need to know if James has mentioned anything to you recently. Was he worried about something, for instance? Has anyone been in touch with him, possibly making excessive demands of him?"

"No. Not that he's told me about."

"I doubt if he'd tell you anything along those lines anyway, secretive little shit!" Josie mumbled with a tut.

"Mum, if you've got nothing nice to say, keep your mouth shut. I can do without this stress." Sienna winced and doubled over.

*Oh fuck! Here we go again!* "Are you okay? Is it the baby, Sienna?"

She stared at Sara and nodded. "I think my waters just broke."

Her mother rushed towards her and flung her arm around Sienna's shoulder. "Don't just sit there, call an ambulance. They've been monitoring the baby regularly as he had an iffy heartbeat. They told us to ring them as soon as her waters broke. I'm calling a halt to these questions. This baby's life is in jeopardy if we don't get her to the hospital now."

Carla removed her phone from her pocket. "I'm on it." She stepped out of the room and reported back a few seconds later. "They're on their way, another five minutes."

"We need to time the contractions," Josie instructed.

Sara was out of her depth. She'd never had to deal with a birth before, and quite frankly, she was crapping herself. *Hurry up, paramedics, please.*

Josie helped her daughter to control her breathing and timed the contractions. Sara, on the other hand, sat there, unfamiliar with what to say or do in the circumstances. She glanced over at Carla who stood rigid and shrugged.

Thankfully, the ambulance arrived within a few minutes as they were situated on the edge of town, close to the hospital. Two paramedics barged into the room after Carla let them in.

"Stand back, we'll take over. Have you timed the contractions?"

"I tried. I lost count, I'm sorry," Josie replied, tears streaming down her face.

Sara placed an arm around Josie's shoulder. "You did your best. I was no use at all, I'm sorry."

"Thanks. We need to get her to hospital, and quickly," Josie told the paramedics, explaining why.

"Let's assess the situation before we move her. It might be too late," the paramedic replied.

"Oh God, don't say that..." Sienna groaned, the pain overwhelming her again.

Sara's knees suddenly felt weak, and she had a struggle remaining on her feet. The fear etched on Sienna's face would live with her forever, she just knew it. "We should go. Leave you in expert hands."

"No...what about James?" Sienna demanded. She howled then and doubled over again.

"This baby isn't going to wait. We'll need to make the preparations for a home birth."

"Oh no. Okay, I'll get some towels." Josie raced out of the room.

Sara stepped back and stood alongside Carla. "Do you know what to do in this instance?"

"Do I heck!" Carla replied. "We shouldn't be here, it's a personal thing, Sara."

"I know. I tried to get away before, but Sienna is concerned about James, rightly so, even though her thoughts should be with the baby now."

"It's a tough call. I'd hate to be in her shoes, on both counts. Crikey, I would never want to go through that pain!"

"Mum always tells me it's a pain you forget. Hard to frigging imagine, if you ask me," Sara whispered.

Josie came bustling back into the room, carrying a large pile of towels. "Don't just stand there, make yourselves useful," she snapped at them.

"How? We're out of our depth, sorry. We're going to shoot off, leave you to it. Good luck, Sienna. We'll be in touch soon, I promise." Sara tugged on Carla's arm, and they escaped the house before anyone could stop them.

"Wow, that was brave of you."

"I was beginning to feel sick in there. It's not part of our job to oversee something like that. It was better to leave the experienced paramedics dealing with the situation. Anyway, we have urgent work to do, trying to locate James Stanley."

Carla released the breath she'd been holding in. "I hear you. Bloody relief to be out of there. Glad you didn't force me to stick around. I think I might have passed out if I'd been forced to witness the actual birth. I don't do pain very well. Why do women put themselves through that? Half the kids I see in the street near me are constantly being shouted at by their mothers, what gives?"

"Don't expect me to be able to shed any light on family life, I have a loyal cat, remember. She's as kind to me as I am to her, never has temper tantrums or throws her food across the room."

"What does that make us, wimps?"

"I'm willing to agree to that. Blimey, I'm dreading Mark and I having the baby conversation in the future. Genuinely, I'm not sure I'd ever cope devoting my life to kids. I have to take my hat off to all the mothers out there who are prepared to go through that pain and anguish. Okay, subject closed, let's concentrate on the task at hand."

"I agree with you. We'll leave the childbirth to those who can stand nine months of discomfort and a lifetime of not having a life of their own to contend with."

Sara punched Emma Wyatt's address into the satnav and expelled a heavy sigh. "I'm getting weary now."

"Me, too. We'd better buck our ideas up if we're gonna tackle her, though, if she's there."

"That's true."

Emma lived out in the country, a road tucked away in Stretton Sugwas. The house was a quaint thatched cottage, the front garden full of shrubs in full bloom, waving in the evening breeze that had suddenly appeared. Sara rang the bell.

The front door was eventually opened by an older gentleman with a rotund stomach. He frowned and looked them up and down with disdain. "If you're Jehovah's Witnesses you can get lost. We don't do any form of religion in this house."

"We're not." Sara flashed her warrant card in his face. "DI Sara Ramsey, and this is my partner, DS Carla Jameson. And you're Mr Wyatt, I take it?"

"Guess again. I'm Ben Masterton."

"I see. Does Emma Wyatt live here, sir?"

"She does. What do you want with her?"

"We'd like to ask her a few questions, if it's convenient."

"It's not. What about?"

Anger burnt her insides. "We'll tell her that, Mr Masterton, if you wouldn't mind getting her for me."

"We're having our evening meal, you'll have to come back another time."

"I get the impression you're shunning us, sir. Do you have something to hide?"

"Think what you like. Sit in your car for ten minutes and come back when we've finished our meal. Nothing interrupts that, not after my wife has slaved half the day preparing it for us, got that?" He closed the door.

"Loud and clear, arsehole." Sara nudged Carla, and they returned to the car. "Let's check in with Craig and Will, see what they've discovered." She rang Craig's number. "It's only me, can you talk?"

"Yes, we're on our way back to the station, boss."

"Any news?"

"We've visited the two men. Aaron Thornton was very amenable, but Brad Iverson was a bit of a tosser. He told us to do one."

"What? Did you tell them about the two men's deaths?"

"Umm…I decided against the idea, boss. Instead, I asked them if they'd been contacted by Douglas Connor recently. Aaron seemed a bit dippy, a little twitchy, if you like. Whereas Brad appeared to be putting on a big 'I am' type of façade. Maybe that was because he had a bird with him. Told me to get out of his face and stop hassling him. I was doing nothing of the sort, by the way."

"I know the type. Bastard. Oh well, if anything happens to him then he's only got himself to blame, hasn't he? We're waiting outside Emma's house. They're eating their meal, and the man of the house made it clear that we weren't welcome to join them. One thing, we believe the perpetrator has got his next victim."

"Oh shit! Who?"

"James Stanley was abducted from outside the pub where he works. We've got the make and colour of the van, no plate number, though. And get this, we just went to break the news to his girlfriend, and she went into bloody labour. What're the odds on that?"

"That's a shitstorm in a teacup, excuse the language, boss."

"You're excused. If James Stanley winds up dead at least she'll have had the baby. Warped way of looking at things, but you get my drift. According to Sienna's mother, James is a prick towards his girlfriend, unconfirmed by her, though."

"There's a response to that, but I'll keep it to myself. All right if we head home after we get back to the station, boss?"

"Got a hot date, have you, Craig?"

"No chance of that. Just going for a few pints with the lads."

"Go, enjoy yourselves. Send the rest of the team home as well while you're at it. Carla and I will see where the land lies here and then call it a day."

"Rightio, see you bright and early tomorrow."

"You will." She ended the call and looked back at the house to see Ben Masterton standing with the front door open. "Okay, we're on. I hope this goes well. I have a feeling he's going to give us a rough ride, calling on them at this time of night."

"Evening," Carla corrected. "Tough shit. We've got a job to do. An innocent person would understand that, wouldn't they?"

"You'd think so. Let's go, see what information they want to feed us. If Emma is there then I don't know what we're going to do."

"They could all be in on it or it's possible that we've made a big mistake and this is all a huge coincidence."

Sara angled her head and asked, "Seriously, is that what you believe?"

"No. I was merely playing devil's advocate for a second or two there, stepping into your shoes for a split second."

"Maybe they've paid a hitman to knock the men off."

They left the car and returned to the house.

Ben grudgingly smiled at them, either that or he had a bout of wind. "Come in. Sorry about earlier, nothing comes between me and my food, not even the police."

"Fair enough. Is Emma home?" Sara asked and stepped over the threshold with Carla.

"Yes, she's in the lounge with my wife and granddaughter." He closed the front door and motioned for them to join him.

The cottage had a warm, cosy atmosphere. The lounge had two major beams and a welcoming inglenook fireplace that was decorated with several bunches of flowers at this time of year instead of a roaring open fire.

Sara smiled at the two women staring at her. The younger woman, who she presumed to be Emma, was holding a child on her lap.

"Hello, there. Sorry to interrupt your evening, everyone."

"This is DI Ramsey and DS Jameson," Ben Masterton announced.

Sara was taken aback slightly that he'd remembered their names.

"Take a seat," Masterton instructed.

Sara and Carla sat on the end of the couch where Emma was sitting.

"What's this about?" the young woman asked, hugging her daughter.

"Maybe it would be better if we discussed this without your daughter being present, Emma."

Emma turned to face her mother and stepfather, her brow tugging into a deep frown. "Why?"

"There are just some things I don't think a child should hear, that's all."

Mrs Masterton rose from her chair. "Come on, little one, it's time for your bath." She reached for the child's hand, but the girl flung her arms around her mother's neck and refused to let go.

"Now, Tia, come on, we have to go."

"Go with Nanny, sweetheart. I won't be long here. I'll join you shortly, I promise."

"I'm scared, Mummy. I don't like these people."

Sara and Carla both smiled at the child in an effort to put her at ease.

Mrs Masterton unhitched the child's arms from her daughter's neck and tickled her. "Come on, munchkin."

The child nattered away as her grandmother successfully carried her from the room.

"So, what's this all about?" Ben demanded.

"Have you been here all evening, Emma?" Sara asked.

"What's that supposed to mean?" Emma retorted.

"Have you?"

"Yes. All day. I haven't stepped foot outside the bloody door in days, except to take Tia to a friend's house for playtime and to nursery, of course. Why? I don't understand what's going on. Why you're here, demanding answers."

"Where were you on Monday evening of this week?"

"Here."

"And Wednesday evening?"

"Again, here. Why? Are you going to tell me why you're asking me?"

"Because a few incidents have occurred this week that we're investigating."

"What type of incidents?" Ben growled.

"Attacks on men. Actually, worse than that, two men have been murdered and one man has also been abducted this evening."

Emma's head jutted forward, and her eyes enlarged. "What, and you think I have something to do with all this? Are you crazy? Why come here and pick on me?"

"Here's the thing, the men in question have a connection to you."

"What sort of connection? None of this is making any sense."

"Spit it out, Inspector, stop going round and round in circles." Ben's voice rose a notch, along with his frustration levels.

"Okay, here's what we're dealing with. We're aware of an incident which took place five years ago—"

"You mean when she was raped!"

"Dad! Did you have to put it like that?" Emma shouted at her stepfather.

He shrugged. "Why not say it how it is? Why skirt around the bloody truth? I'm sick of doing it, walking on eggshells. I've had to bite my tongue for bloody years. No more, I say, no more. Let's get the facts out there. The bloody police did nothing back then, and now you're on our doorstep, why? Because something has happened to these men after all this time and she's your number one suspect. Give me fucking strength. Have you seen the size of her? Have you? As if a tiny mite like that could overpower those thugs." He paced the room, anxiously running a hand over his balding head.

"Please, Mr Masterton, you're not doing either of you any favours by getting worked up. We're here to ask a few questions. No one is accusing anyone of doing anything right now."

"I'm sorry. She's been through such a lot over the years. You have no idea the trauma those…those animals put her through. And what happened to them? They got off with all the charges. All of them. How can a group of men do that to a young innocent girl of eighteen and be allowed to get away with it?"

"It's hard to fathom, I grant you that, sir. Emma, have you had any form of contact with the men involved in the incident since it happened?"

"No, I mean, yes. There was the court case I was subjected to, in which they got off. That was the last time I laid eyes on them, I swear. Are you telling me that some of the men are dead?"

"That's right. Two, Douglas Connor and Wesley Bowen."

Emma shuddered as if hearing the names brought the memory of that dreadful night flooding back. "Honestly, you have to believe me. Why would I go after the men after all this time? It doesn't make sense." Her hands shook. She clenched them together and thrust them between her legs.

"That's right. Why would she?" Ben added. He pointed at Sara, his hand shaking a touch. "She's not the sort. All her attention is on that child now. Rearing her to be a courageous and happy individual."

"I see. Are you telling me that none of the men from that gang have ever tried to make contact with you over the years?"

"No, never. I would have called the police if they'd tried to harass me."

"What about your daughter, Emma?"

"What about her? Are you telling me you think she's behind these killings? Are you insane?"

"No, sorry, that's not what I meant at all. Is she the product of that night?"

Emma's head plummeted to her chest, and she mumbled, "Yes. Although she isn't aware of what went on. I told her, well, that her father was dead."

"When did you tell her that?"

"A few years ago. She was two, almost three at the time. She kept pestering me to see her daddy. Broke my bloody heart in two, that did. Those monsters ruined my life. She's a constant reminder of the… I try not to persecute her for that, but it's so hard at times. She looks like him."

"Which one?"

"I'd rather not say. It's too painful for me to say his name."

"I understand. The last thing I want to do is back you into a corner and force the issue, however, if you suspect you know who the father is, I think it would be a good idea if you told us."

"Why?" Ben jumped to his stepdaughter's defence. "I'm not liking what I'm hearing here. You come in here demanding to know where Emma has been on three separate nights, and now you're sitting there, forcing her to relive the worst ruddy moment of her entire life in such a blasé fashion. Do you have any idea of the distress, strain and suffering rape victims have to go through? That night pales into insignificance after a while, it's the hurt it leaves behind that destroys the victim's soul. Yes, she's had Tia to bring up, but the damage that night has caused to Emma's ability to get out there into the world…well, take my word for it, she gets stressed even going a mile out of the village. No chance in this lifetime or the next of her ever holding down a job. Her confidence sucks, all because of those bastards. They should have been thrown in prison for decades, instead they were set free. Why? Because the system is corrupt. Because their parents could afford decent legal representation and we couldn't at the time."

"I'm sorry you feel that way, Mr Masterton, that you feel the system has failed you. Look, I wouldn't be doing my job right if I didn't come here and make enquiries into your stepdaughter's whereabouts this week."

"Why? I don't get why you should pick on her. Do you know for a fact that what these guys did was a bloody one-off? Have you looked into that possibility?"

"Not yet, but we will."

He flung an arm up in the air. "Jesus, call yourself a detective? Go detect things instead of coming here accusing Emma of something she isn't capable of doing, for Christ's sake."

"I wasn't aware that I'd accused Emma or anything of the sort. I'm conducting a line of enquiry that I believe is relevant to my investigation, sir. If you wouldn't mind remaining calm, it will make this a darn sight easier. Either that or I can take Emma down to the station for questioning, if that's the way you'd rather have it. Either way, I have a right to be here, to ask your stepdaughter questions relating to an incident which might have led to two men's deaths." Sara's cheeks warmed under Masterton's glare. She could tell how irate he was getting and regretted her choice of words as soon as they were aired. She prepared herself for a battle.

"No, I refute that. What you're here to do is accuse Emma of killing those two men when she's barely stepped outside her front door in months. How on earth would she even begin to find out where those bastards live, for instance? All she's guilty of is trying to get on with her broken life the best way she knows how to. I'll let you into a secret that is going to blow your mind, Inspector. That child up there—"

Emma hid her head in her hands. "Dad, please, don't say any more."

"They need to know, love."

"We do," Sara insisted. "You were going to tell us about the child, sir?"

"I was and I will. Emma, I'm sorry if this upsets you, they have a right to know about this, love."

Emma sobbed.

The atmosphere suddenly descended into a darkness Sara hadn't anticipated coming.

"She rejected the child at first, all because of those blasted men. There, I've said it," Masterton announced, staring at Emma.

She wailed and rocked back and forth in her chair.

Sara slid along the couch and laid a hand on Emma's knee. "Is that right?"

"Yes, it's true…but I love her now. Please, don't hold that against me." Sobs broke up her sentences.

"I won't. I'm sure a lot of women who went through a similar ordeal would have the same feelings you experienced, love. You mustn't feel bad."

"Unless you've been through such humiliation and trauma, you'll never know what those men did to me. The memories are choking me right now. That night has come flooding back since you arrived. I'm not in a good place. I want to help you with your enquiries, but I can't." Her words were muffled by the hands over her face.

"It's okay. We didn't mean to evoke such horrendous memories for you, I promise. Can you understand our need to be here, though?"

"I suppose so. You have to believe me when I say I know nothing about these men's deaths. I wouldn't be strong enough mentally to cope with such a thing. I'm not the sort to seek revenge, I wouldn't have it in me. You have to believe me."

"I do. Please, can you help us then? Think back to that time, to what the men said to you. Did any of them intimate that they had hurt another woman before, in the way they hurt you?"

She remained still and silent for a few moments and then shook her head. She lowered her hands to reveal a river of tears streaming down her flushed cheeks. "No, I can't recall them saying anything like that. All they said that evening…well…they called me a bunch of names, whore, slapper, slag, that sort of thing, and yet they were the ones taking advantage of me against my will, so what did that make them then?"

"I'm so sorry you had to go through that disgusting act and that the men got off with the crime they committed. You said it was obvious who the father was. Have you ever contacted him about it?"

"No. Dad," she looked up at her stepfather, "he told me to forget it, that we would struggle to make ends meet if we had to, we didn't need a rapist's money to bring up Tia."

"On the one hand I agree with your stepfather, on the other, you're entitled to maintenance money from him. It might go a long way to easing your pain, love."

"I doubt it. Anyway, it's too late now."

"How so?"

"You told me he's already dead."

Sara tilted her head. "Was it Douglas or Wesley?"

"The first one. She's the spitting image of him. Well, I think she is anyway."

"Then his parents have a right to know," Sara pushed gently.

"No frigging way!" Ben shouted, infuriated by the obscene suggestion.

"I'm sorry, but they do. Whether you think I'm in the right or wrong suggesting that, they can't be held responsible for their son's sickening actions."

"There you've hit the nail on the head, sickening actions. We'd rather not have those people in our lives. Do you have any idea what that could do to Emma? How unstable it could make her? There's a possibility she could reject little Tia again, none of us want that."

"Then what's the solution? Those people are grieving their loss. Knowing that their son has a daughter might be the tonic they need to hear right now."

Ben marched across the room and stood before Sara. He pointed at her and then wagged his finger. "You tell that family and I'll report you to your superiors. You have no right to divulge this information."

"I think you'll find I have every right. You're misunderstanding my motive, Mr Masterton. You cannot hold the grandparents responsible for their son's behaviour in his younger days."

Masterton swivelled on his heel and marched across the other side of the room to the patio doors overlooking the rear garden. "You're wrong, so wrong. If you tell them you'll be ripping this family apart. Don't do it to us, to Emma, I'm begging you."

His words were heartfelt and touched Sara. "I can't promise that I won't do it. What I can say is that I will run it past my superior, see where we stand legally. The last thing I'd want is to put Emma in an awkward position." She patted Emma on the knee.

Emma offered her a weak smile in return. "Thank you. I'm not sure I could take them interfering in my life, not at this time."

"Why do you say that, Emma?"

Emma swallowed, and her head dipped again. "I've not been well lately."

"I'm sorry to hear that. Do you mind telling me what's been wrong with you?"

"It's none of your damn business, leave the girl alone," Masterton blasted across the room.

His tone held a warning that shook Sara. "Emma? Can you tell me?"

"I was sectioned a few months ago."

"Oh, I see. Can I ask why?"

The fingers of her right hand circled the back of her left one. "I…" She flipped her left arm over and pulled her sleeve back to reveal a mixture of new and old scars etched into her wrists.

"You didn't?" Sara gasped.

"Yes, I couldn't stand it any more. Those men have a lot to answer for. No one knows the damage it does to the victim's head. Most nights I only manage to get an hour or two's sleep. Do you have any sense of how draining that can be when you have a boisterous four-year-old to contend with?"

"I can only imagine. I'm so sorry, Emma, have you sought help? Had counselling perhaps?"

"Every year since it happened. The counsellors haven't got a clue. They bamboozle me with reasons why I should get on with my life. It's been five years, they keep telling me, don't they think I know how long it's been? Five years, two months and seven days to be precise, and it never gets easier. The pain I felt that night in my head and down below will remain with me. The distress of bearing a child to one of those morons is a constant reminder of what I went through during a disgusting experience. Every time I look at her…Jesus, I wanted rid of everything. Inside, I'm dead anyway, I have been since it happened. Most people think of it as a simple act, a misjudgement on the perpetrator's part. In truth, they forget it is a violation of another human being. No one can ever right that wrong, and yet victims are supposed to just pick themselves up and get on with their lives as if nothing ever occurred. I need to go, to rid myself of these feelings of worthlessness."

Tears pricked Sara's eyes, and her throat burned with acid. "Me apologising isn't enough, I know. There must be someone out there who can help you, sweetheart. Perhaps discussing how you feel with other victims will benefit you to balance things out. I can do some research, find a support group in the area. I'm sure there must be one, somewhere."

"Thank you. It's too late. I hate my life, what I've become since…"

"Emma, don't say that. We do our very best for you. We appreciate how difficult all this has been for you. Have we ever let you down in the past?" Ben asked.

"No. I'm sorry, Dad. Sorry that you've had to hear all of this. Maybe it was time for me to reveal the truth."

Sara nodded. "If this is the first time you've said it out loud to your family, then yes, I believe you're on the right path to getting better, Emma."

"Are you an expert, Inspector?" Ben snapped and moved to stand next to his stepdaughter.

"No. But I have the experience of life behind me, a life which has known much pain and grief. Believe me, my words aren't as worthless as you might think they are, sir."

His eyes narrowed. Her words had challenged him, and by the look of things, he wasn't used to women doing that in this house. "Have you finished your questions now?"

"Yes, I believe I have. I'm going to leave you a card, Emma. Give me a ring if you can think of anything else we might have overlooked this evening. The fact remains that two men have already lost their lives and another one has been reported missing."

"I repeat, this has nothing to do with Emma. It's time you left,

Inspector. Let Emma get on with her life, knowing that two, possibly three, of her attackers can no longer hurt her or another woman in the same abhorrent way."

"Not the way I would look at it, or their families come to that, but everyone is entitled to their opinion."

"That's right, it's a free country, and furthermore, I can say what I like in my own house. I'll show you to the door."

Sara let the stepfather leave the room and then leaned in and whispered, "Are you safe here?"

Emma gasped. "Yes. He's a pussycat really. All he's guilty of is protecting me. Those men…they're the animals, and I agree with Dad, they deserve everything they got and more for what they did to me. I'm just sorry it took someone so long to have the courage to do what I've been thinking about doing for years."

"And I don't blame you having those thoughts. My advice would be to keep them to yourself for now, while the investigation is in full flow, otherwise people might misconstrue your meaning."

"No problem there. I have no freedom, I rarely go out, because of what they did to me."

"So we gather. Thanks for speaking with us, Emma. Take care of yourself and your beautiful daughter."

"I will. Good luck with solving your case. I'm sorry I couldn't be of help."

Ben showed up at the doorway again and demanded, "Are you coming?"

Sara and Carla left the room and found him holding the front door open for them. Sara suspected he was restraining himself as his face had turned the colour of a ripe tomato.

Sara smiled as she passed him. "Thanks for allowing us in this evening, sir."

"Whatever. Don't come back. She knows nothing. Let her live her life in peace." With that, he slammed the door in their faces.

"Charming!" Sara seethed as she walked towards the car with Carla.

"What do you make of him?" Carla asked once they were tucked up in the car.

"Don't tempt me, I could come up with a few choice words."

"Me, too. There's something about him, though, did you feel it?"

Sara faced her and slotted the key in the ignition. "You think he knows more about this than he's letting on?"

"I'm getting that impression. What do we know about him?"

"Not much. Let's rectify that in the morning. It's almost nine, and I'm dead on my feet. Want me to drop you off at home or drive back to the station to pick up your car?"

"Sorry, back to the station, if that's okay? I feel bad as you're going out of your way."

"Nonsense. There's hardly any traffic at this time of night, it's all good. If you know a shortcut, give me a shout and I'll take it."

Sara dropped Carla off at the station ten minutes later. The drive back to her house added yet another twenty minutes to her long day. She'd called ahead, told Mark to expect her soon, in the hope he'd have the dinner ready for her when she got home. She smiled as she turned the corner and saw him standing on the doorstep, cuddling Misty.

"Hello, you two, how's it going?"

Mark bent down to kiss her. "We're fine. How are you? Another long day at the office."

Sara wasn't taken aback by his words, it wasn't a criticism, at least that's not how it had registered with her. "I know. The days are getting longer. I need to reassess that. It was important Carla and I stop off to question someone loosely connected with the crime. Shit! You don't need to hear this. What's for dinner?"

"I'm always here if you need to vent, you know that, love."

"I know and I love you for it. Why are you avoiding the question about dinner?"

He laughed, and she fell in love all over again.

"I wasn't aware that I had, sorry. I've knocked up a chicken pasta bake. I have no idea what it's going to be like, so don't expect much. It was one of those 'shove it all in a dish and see how it turns out' concoctions."

Sara put her nose in the air. "Well, it smells delicious, and I'm starving, so bring it on." She ruffled Misty's head and kissed it.

They entered the house and drifted into the kitchen. Mark had already laid the table, and there were two glasses of red wine poured out.

"You read my mind. I definitely need that tonight. I don't even have the energy to get changed."

"Sit. You don't have to do a thing, just eat and drink, I'll do everything else."

"You're amazing. What did I do to deserve a man like you sharing my life?"

"Get away with you. Let me dish up. You'll probably regret saying that if this goes belly up. I'm worried about the pasta drying out and becoming hard."

"Don't worry, I'm sure it'll be delicious."

And it was, in spite of Mark's reservations.

Sara tumbled into bed at around ten-thirty, a little light-headed from the bottle of wine they'd consumed between them. She drifted off to sleep not long after.

## 8

Hunter wasn't happy. He hated James Stanley. Since he'd captured the shithead, he'd driven him potty. Hadn't given him a moment's peace.

At first, he'd come across all cocky, but overnight, especially during the night, he'd turned into a snivelling wreck of a man and the fucker hadn't slept, which meant that Hunter, having shared the same room with him, hadn't managed to grab any shuteye either. Even when he'd brought Tyson in to sit with them. If anything, thinking about it, maybe that's what had made Stanley a darn sight worse.

"You're pitiful. So full of crap. Call yourself a man?" he scolded Stanley.

"I'm sorry. I'm scared. Can you let me go? I'm sorry for what I did. I promise I'll spend the rest of my life being remorseful."

"Stop whining, it's all going to be over soon. To be honest, I'm bored with you."

"What? What are you going to do to me?"

Hunter sat opposite Stanley. "Where would be the fun in me telling you that, eh?"

"Are you sure there's nothing I can do?"

"Nope. You've had five years to put things right. Instead, you're guilty of making things a whole lot worse. The court might have accepted the part you played as an innocent one, I can't, you're all as guilty as each other. Here's a fact I bet you don't know. She had a child because of what you five put her through that night."

Stanley's mouth hung open, revealing several silver fillings at the rear. He shook his head in disbelief. "No! I don't believe you."

Hunter flew at him and smashed his fist into the stunned man's face. "Don't call me a liar. You might've got away with calling her one five years ago, but it won't wash with me, you hear me, scumbag?"

With his hands still tied behind his back, Stanley wiped the blood mixed with snot on the shoulder of his jacket. "Shit! That hurt!"

"It was nothing compared to what's going to happen to you. Get up." Hunter yanked Stanley to his feet.

He toppled slightly on the spot, his legs still bound at the ankle.

Tyson growled and stared at the man from his position by the door.

"What are you going to do with me?"

"You'll find out soon. Now shut the fuck up, I've heard enough from you." Hunter flicked open his penknife.

Stanley flinched and held his head away from him. Hunter bent down and cut the rope from his ankles. While Hunter was down there, a vile stench filled his nostrils.

He stood upright again and got in Stanley's face. "You filthy bastard, you've shat yourself."

"I didn't have any other option. I'm sorry. I tried to tell you I wanted to go to the toilet during the night. You ignored me, what was I supposed to do?"

"Fecking twat! Hold on to it, like any normal person would."

"I couldn't. This isn't a normal situation. I'm scared out of my mind, worried about what you're going to do to me."

"Worry no more, shithead! Because all will be revealed soon enough."

"What are you talking about?"

"Questions, questions, don't you ever fucking shut up? I kept the other two with me for a day or two, got to know them a little better before I did the deed. I know all I want to know about you and I can't stand the sight of you any longer. You're doomed, mate." He tugged Stanley's arm, spinning him on the spot and pushed him towards the door to the cabin.

Tyson inched forward, one leg at a time, his lip curled up in a snarl as he drooled.

"Down boy, you'll get your chance."

Stanley tried to wriggle out of Hunter's grasp, but he held firm, digging his fingers into the flesh of his arm. "No. You can't do this."

"Don't tell me what I can and can't do, it won't end well, buster." Hunter clicked his fingers, instructing Tyson to come to heel by his side. It took two attempts. The dog was already homing in on his target and visibly salivating at the prospect.

"I don't want to do this. Please, won't you reconsider? I have a baby on the way. It's due any minute. I want to see my child. Please, let me do that. You can do what you like after the baby is born."

"Unbelievable. You think you're in a position to barter with me? Who do you think I am?" Hunter opened the front door, shoved Stanley ahead of him and aimed towards the van. He threw Stanley in the back and then ordered Tyson to get in there with him.

Tyson pinned Stanley in position, snarling as he stood over him.

"Shit! Get him off me!"

"Keep still and he won't do anything. Piss him off, mate, and he'll sink his teeth in. He's a trained killer, just so you know."

"What? But..." Stanley fell silent when Tyson growled.

Hunter chuckled and reversed the van. He drove down the track to the main road. Not long after, he pulled into Sharmon Forest on the edge of Hereford. He hadn't been here since he was a kid so had forgotten the lay of the land. That didn't bother him. If anything, it added to his excitement. He parked the car and removed the holdall full of equipment from the footwell on the passenger side. Then he opened the back door and clicked his fingers to beckon Tyson. The dog instantly freed Stanley from his awkward position.

"Get out," he ordered. "We're going on an adventure."

"I don't want to. All I want to do is go home to see my girlfriend."

"You have three seconds or I send Tyson back in there with no restrictions."

Stanley shot out of the van on the count of two.

"Walk."

Stanley frowned. "Where to?"

He pointed at the forest ahead of them. "In there. Where no one will see us."

Stanley took a few steps backwards. Tyson sensed he was about to run, pounced and sank his teeth into Stanley's leg.

"Get him off me!"

"Are you going to behave?"

"Yes. I'm sorry, you have my word."

"Leave it, Tyson."

The dog immediately pulled away from Stanley but remained within striking distance to act as a warning.

"Now move."

Wincing, Stanley trudged towards the wooded area.

"Up the pace and stop trying my patience, you fucking moron."

His captive walked faster for a few steps and then slowed again. Hunter dropped the bag on the ground and unzipped it to reveal his rifle. He hadn't wanted to show his hand so early, but this guy was deliberately pissing him off now. He dug the muzzle in Stanley's back.

"Get moving, arsehole."

"I don't want to die." Stanley sniffled.

"You won't, not if you can outrun me and Tyson." Hunter laughed.

He kept a close eye behind him, making sure no one else pulled into the car park. The overhead trees blocked out the morning sun, giving the area an eerie feel that was fitting for what Hunter had in mind. Tyson stared up at him now and again, awaiting further instructions. He knew what was expected of him and was eager to please his master.

Stanley stumbled. "Get up and watch where you're stepping. You'd do well to think about that going forward, mate."

"What are you talking about?" His captive's voice had grown weak now, as if he was resigned to what lay ahead of him.

"Move it and shut up." He prodded the rifle in the small of Stanley's back.

They progressed deeper into the area until Hunter felt they had gone far enough. "Stop, this will do." He withdrew his penknife from his pocket and cut through the rope tying Stanley's wrists together. "There, I'm a fair man. I wouldn't want you to think otherwise."

"Fair? You're going to hunt me down and you call that being *fair*?"

Hunter lashed out with the barrel of his rifle. Stanley's jaw took the brunt of the force, and the sound of crunching bone echoed through the trees.

Stanley screamed. "Jesus!" he managed to muffle the words.

"I've told you a dozen times or more to shut the fuck up, now, maybe you'll listen to me, right?"

Stanley nodded.

"Okay, here we go then. The aim of the game is that I give you a two-minute head start. Make the most of it, it's really not long in a strange place where you can't get your bearings. After the two minutes are up, we come after you."

"We? You mean the dog?"

"Of course. How dumb are you? As you've already witnessed, he's dying to sink his teeth into your flesh." He tipped his head back and roared.

"You're sick!" Stanley muttered, holding the side of his jaw with his right hand as the fear emerged in his eyes.

Hunter grinned. "Now you know what it's like to feel utter terror. You're going to take that reaction to your grave, moron. You shouldn't have violated Emma. She didn't deserve it, no one deserves to be humiliated and degraded the way your gang set out to do. She's a hundred times better than any of you. You will be punished until you die, so make good speed, mate. Tyson and I are experienced hunters. Now run, time's a wasting as they say."

Stanley didn't need to be told twice. He bolted through the trees, tripping a few times and bumping into several trees due to him constantly looking over his shoulder. "Help me! Please, help me, someone."

## Run For Your Life

Hunter couldn't help laughing at the escapee's pleas. His stopwatch had been set; it reached ninety seconds. "Sod it, go find him, Tyson. Do your worst, boy, I'll be right behind you."

By now, Stanley had disappeared, the forest shielding him with its thickness. It was only the sound of the man's ridiculous pleading that highlighted his position.

Tyson's barking ahead of him told Hunter that his devoted dog had tracked down the man. He whistled to call the Rottweiler off. Tyson returned to his heel. Stanley was lying on the ground, a gaping wound in his side where Tyson had attacked.

"You gave in too easily. We're going to give you another chance. Another two minutes, get up."

"I can't, I'm done. Do what you have to do to me."

Hunter shrugged and aimed at the man's arm. "No skin off my nose, bud." He squeezed the trigger, releasing a bullet which hit Stanley's forearm.

He yelled and writhed on the forest floor.

"Last chance, either you get up and run or I set Tyson on you again. Is that the way you prefer to go out? Being mauled to death by an angry dog?"

"No. Okay, can you help me get to my feet?"

Hunter tutted and held out an arm.

His captive tugged hard enough to hoist himself onto his feet. He winced and clutched his side, blood seeping through his fingers. "I won't be able to run very fast, not with my injuries."

"Tough shit! Get to it. I'll give you an extra minute this time." He set his stopwatch and grinned.

Stanley took off again, his steps laboured due to the blood loss he had already incurred.

Adrenaline emerged and crammed Hunter's veins. "I'm going to enjoy this one more than the others. Boy, you'll get your chance after I've had my fun. Wait there."

Again, Stanley dipped out of view, and for the second time, Hunter went against his promise and set off early, this time with Tyson by his side. They weaved through the trees and finally tracked their prey down a few minutes later. Hunter aimed and shot him in the right leg. The man yelled out and hobbled, doing his best to remain upright. Hunter lined up another shot, and this time Stanley went down as the bullet sank into the same leg.

But seconds later, Stanley bounced to his feet again and took off.

"Okay, boy, go get him!"

Tyson barked a response and bolted after his quarry.

Stanley must have heard the dog close behind him. He glanced round briefly and cried out. Tyson jumped at his back. It didn't take much to topple Stanley to the ground. Hunter took a leisurely stroll towards them, a satisfied grin stretching his lips apart.

*Another one down, only two to go, and I've got something special awaiting them.*

## 9

Sara received the urgent call on her way into work the following morning. "Hi, Lorraine, I'm on my way to the station, can you ring me there in a few minutes?"

"Nope. You need to make a detour."

"I do? Shit! Don't tell me you've found James Stanley."

"Umm…yes, that's right, and it ain't pretty. Whoever is guilty of doing this is notching it up a level each time. I'm not going to say more, you can see for yourself what I mean, later."

"Why me? Ugh…I can do without this fucking crap right now. Okay, tell me where you are."

"A new one on me, it's Sharmon Forest. You can look it up on the map, it's out near Holme Lacy."

"Christ, okay. I'll get in touch with Carla and meet you over there. TTFN."

"Bye."

"Siri, ring Carla's number."

The phone rang.

"Are you checking up on me? I'm running a few minutes late, nothing major. Sorry."

"No, stop jumping to conclusions. Lorraine has just called me.

She's found James Stanley in Sharmon Forest, do you know where that is?"

"I think so, Holme Lacy way, isn't it?"

"Yep, can you meet me there?"

"I haven't got enough petrol in the car. I was going to fill up, but we were running late. Forget that, I'll call into Sainsbury's and get some. As you were. I'll join you when I can."

"You are funny."

"What? You shouldn't ask tricky questions first thing in the morning when I'm not fully awake."

Sara laughed. "I wasn't aware that I had. See you soon."

She had rung ahead and told Lorraine what time to expect her. Her pathologist friend told her she'd meet her in the car park as the crime scene was a little hard to locate.

There were two police cars already in attendance, and the uniformed officers were busy cordoning off the entrance. She waved, recognising a couple of them.

While Sara waited for Lorraine to come and meet her, she slipped on her protective suit. Carla pulled up a few minutes later, before Lorraine arrived.

Sara threw Carla a suit. "Good of you to join me. Actually, you did well to get here so soon."

"No one at the pumps, which was a blessing at that time of the morning. What are you waiting for? Not me, I hope? I would've caught you up."

"Nope, I'm under strict instructions to stay here. Lorraine should be here soon. Wait, there she is now. Are you ready?"

"I am. Should we leave our shoe covers off for now?"

"Yep, I think we should. Come on, let's see what state James Stanley is in. According to Lorraine, the crimes appear to be getting worse, so be prepared."

"I don't care what I see out in the field, within reason, that is, but I can't be doing with attending another PM so soon, not after the last one."

"Wuss."

They approached Lorraine. She smiled briefly and motioned for them to join her. They trekked through the dense forest for a good five minutes or so until they reached the other members of Lorraine's team.

"Bloody hell, this is in the back of beyond. Who found the body?" Sara asked, scanning the area, finding it hard to imagine anyone in their right mind coming to this eerie place first thing in the morning. *Each to their own.*

"Another jogger. Don't ask, it's beyond me. Maybe they come here for the peace and solitude. Anyway, he didn't expect to stumble across the deceased, that's for sure. Here's the jogger's card. He started ranting at me when I told him he needed to hang around and speak with you."

"It's no problem, we appreciate people have busy lives, we'll catch up with him later. Can we see the body?"

"Sure. I doubt if you'll want to look at it for long, though."

Sara gulped. "Is it that bad?"

"You can judge that for yourselves. Follow me."

Lorraine led the way a few feet farther and then pointed to the ground. There was no need for her to do that as Sara's gaze was already focused on Stanley's remains. The urge to vomit presented itself, but she managed to push it back down before anything emerged.

"Jesus, that's sick. Has some kind of animal got to him?"

"If I didn't know any better, I would say that a dog was involved in the hunt this time."

"No way! Bloody hell, well, that's just warped."

Lorraine shrugged. "I did warn you. The perp's MO is shifting, getting crueller each time."

"You don't say," Sara replied sarcastically.

Lorraine pulled a face at her.

Sara stared at the victim. His face was unrecognisable, torn to shreds. His nose was there but lying on his cheek, hanging by a thread, and his lips were non-existent. His throat had a gaping wound at the front and on one side.

Carla heaved beside her.

"Take it over there if you're gonna be sick," Lorraine snapped.

Carla rushed to a clearing around five feet away and liberated the contents of her stomach.

Sara felt sorry for her partner and joined her with a packet of tissues she'd produced from her pocket. "Are you okay?"

"You must have a stomach made of iron. How are you not affected by that?"

"I have a stronger resolve than you. Go and sit in the car if you want, I can do the necessary here."

"No, I'm not going to be seen as namby-pamby. I'll be fine now that's out of my system."

"My advice would be not to focus too much on the victim's injuries."

"Hard not to when they're in your face like that. You have to ask yourself what type of fiend we're searching for. There's no way a woman could be responsible for this, is there?"

"Nope, I think we can definitely omit Emma from the equation."

"Yeah, what about her stepfather, though?"

"Let's discuss that when we get back to the station. I need to get Lorraine's thoughts on what we're up against here. She can be insightful at times like this, you know that."

"True enough," Carla agreed.

They rejoined Lorraine who crouched beside the corpse. "We've got a couple of bullet wounds to his leg, both entry and exit wounds. And another gaping wound to his side. His right arm has been savaged, exposing the elbow bone. Looks like the left arm escaped such treatment."

"I'm going out on a limb here, pardon the pun, dare I ask if anything has happened to his genitals? There appears to be a lot of blood in that area, but I can't really tell from here."

Lorraine eased the man's zip apart and peered in. "Yep, his penis is missing. That seems a clean cut to me, probably done by a knife. The same can't be said about his testicles, though. The insides are missing, but the scrotum is still in place."

It was Sara's turn to heave. "Jesus! That's revolting. Can you tell if the wounds were inflicted before or after his death?"

"I'm thinking after, but I'm not too sure. There's far too much blood on his clothes to determine which particular wound it came from, if you get my drift?"

"I do. Either way, the poor man suffered a great deal before he took his last breath."

"No doubt about it," Lorraine confirmed. "Do you need anything else?"

"Umm...I suppose a formal ID would be good. I'm presuming this is James Stanley, but you know where presumption leads us, up shit creek."

"There's an evidence bag over there containing his wallet. I can confirm it's the man you're searching for."

"Okay, do you still need us?"

"No, you go. I'll get my report off to you soon."

"Brilliant, thanks, Lorraine. We'll need to go and tell his girlfriend. We left her yesterday afternoon, giving birth to their baby."

"Bugger, and he'll never get to see it. That's rough, on all of them."

"Yeah, I can't say I'm looking forward to breaking the news. See you later."

Sara trudged back through the forest, her legs heavy with resignation. "Bastard, I really don't want to do this."

"What, go to the hospital?"

"Yeah, I wish there was a way around it, but Sienna has a right to know he's dead."

"Maybe we could postpone it a day or two?"

"I don't know. If we do that and the bosses find out or it comes out in the news, our names are going to be mud."

"Yeah, it's a catch-twenty-two situation, damned if you do and damned if you don't."

Sara sighed and removed her protective suit which she rolled into a ball and threw into the boot of the car. "I'll tell you what, why don't I go to the hospital and you go back to the station, bring the team up to date on what went on last night at Emma's?"

"I was going to suggest the same. Okay, want me to do some digging on Emma's family, her mother and stepfather? I know he was there last night, but he came across as someone with a grudge. Maybe he's paid someone to do this, after all."

Sara contemplated the suggestion for a few seconds. "Possibly. Yes, dig into all their backgrounds and their financials, see if there's been any large withdrawals lately. I suppose working on the same lines, then it's possible Emma could have paid a hitman to do her dirty work for her as well as the stepfather."

"Or her mother even!"

"True enough. See you in an hour or so." Sara jumped in her car and set off. On the drive back into the city, her head was all over the place. This had to be one of her most complex cases to date, and she still wasn't sure in which direction to go for the best.

She was relieved to find a couple of spare spaces to choose from in the hospital car park. She wandered into the reception area and asked, "I need the maternity ward, please? I've not been there before so I don't have a clue what direction it's in."

The redhead behind the desk smiled and pointed at the sign on the wall. The maternity ward was on the second level.

"Thanks very much, that'll teach me to look rather than ask next time."

"No problem. You're not alone, I assure you."

Sara hopped into the lift, which she shared with an elderly couple. The female was wearing a dressing gown and using a metal frame to aid her. The male stared ahead of him, seemingly bored out of his mind. The doors whooshed open.

"You go ahead, dear, we're in no rush," the lady said with a pained expression and a glimmer of a smile.

"Thanks. Have a good day."

"We will," the old man grumbled.

Sara followed the signs to the end of the corridor and turned right towards the maternity ward. She squeezed out a few pumps of hand sanitiser and entered the ward. A couple of nurses were seated at the desk.

One of them glanced up and asked, "Can I help?"

Sara produced her ID. "I know it's not visiting time, I'm here on official business. Is it possible to see Sienna? Oh heck, I've just realised, I don't know her surname."

"That's no problem. It's not a common name. Yes, she's here. The third bed down on the right. I have to ask, is everything okay?"

Sara rolled her eyes. "I have some bad news, and frankly, I'm uncertain how to tell her."

"It's not ideal. She had a rough birth at home yesterday and was brought in by paramedics. She's resting at the moment, although her mother is in there sitting with her. Maybe you should have a quiet word with her first."

"That would be great. Would you mind getting her for me? Only, if Sienna lays eyes on me she'll probably demand to know why I'm here."

"Sure. Wait here. We have a small consultation room available, if you'd like to use that?"

"Excellent, thanks."

"I'll show you where it is and then go and fetch her mother."

The plump nurse left her desk and led Sara to the consultation room. Sara paced the room, mulling over what to say to the woman when she arrived.

The door opened, and a tentative Josie entered. "Oh, hello. When the nurse told me someone was here to see me I got worried. Is everything all right?"

"Hello, Josie, nice to see you again. How are Sienna and the baby doing?"

"They're both fine. She had a little boy, he's a wee gem. Any news on his father? We haven't heard a dicky bird from him."

Sara pointed at the chair in the corner. "Take a seat."

"Oh dear, is it bad news?" She sank into the chair and stared wide-eyed at Sara.

"I'm afraid so. James' body was discovered in a forest first thing this morning. I'm sorry to put this on your shoulders, Josie, I didn't want to barge onto the ward and tell Sienna if she wasn't up to hearing the news."

Josie buried her head in her hands and rocked back and forth in the chair. "Oh my, oh dear. What on earth am I going to tell my daughter? After what she's been through in the past twenty-four hours. That poor little baby, he'll grow up never knowing who his father was."

Sara crouched and rubbed the older woman's arm. "I'm so sorry, there was no easy way to tell you. Can I get you a glass of water?"

Josie released her hands to reveal her tear-stained face. "No, thank you. How did he die? I know I wasn't his biggest fan, but this has come as a shock."

Sara nodded her understanding. "He was murdered. That's three murders we're investigating in this area which have taken place in the past week."

"Three? By the same person? Is that what you're telling me?"

"We believe so. I can't go into details, not until I have the full report from the pathologist in my hands. I'm so sorry. I wanted to tell you first, to get your advice whether Sienna should be told yet or not. It's always difficult at times like this, you know, when someone is in hospital."

"I'm not sure. I want to protect my daughter, but on the other hand, she would want to know if...James has passed away. It's only natural, isn't it?"

"It is. Maybe we could tell her together. Do you think that would be better?"

Josie heaved out a sigh, shrugged and glanced out the tiny window in the room. Looking up at the clouds floating past, she asked, "Do you know why? Had he done something in the past that we should know about?"

"Well, maybe you can tell me what you knew about him first."

"I know he used to beat Sienna. I've tried to get her to leave him in the past, but she was having none of it. I feared for her and the baby. He knocked her senseless a few months ago. I thought she was going to lose the baby."

"My God, I had no idea. Did Sienna report the incident, any of the abuse to the police?"

"No, she refused to."

"Has your daughter ever mentioned anything that might have happened in James's past?"

"No. Do you think she's kept secrets from me?"

"I don't know. I'd really like to question her further, in light of what you've told me."

"I think you should, too. Can you tell me what you know about James?"

Sara nodded and rose to her feet as her legs were aching. She kicked them out to get the circulation flowing again. "We were unaware of the crime he committed until we discovered the second murder victim and made the connection. Sorry, I'm waffling…the thing is, James and four other men were accused of gang raping a young woman five years ago. The case went to court, but the jury found them not guilty."

"Jesus, no, she never told me that. I don't even know if she's aware of it. Bloody hell! I knew there was something off about him. He's the sort to present himself as a kind, genuine type of guy, but behind closed doors, that's when the evil appears. I've seen it fleetingly on occasions, which is why I tried to persuade Sienna to move back home. The bastard! Sorry, but if he was that evil, well…then he deserves to be dead. I'm glad he will no longer be in my daughter's life, and that wee bairn won't know what a wicked shit he was. Yes, that's it, she should definitely know."

Josie stood and marched to the door.

Sara tugged at her arm. "If we tell her, we need to do it gently, not go in there all guns blazing. She loved him, no matter what, we should remember that."

"I'll leave the talking to you. You've had more experience than me with this type of conversation."

Sara smiled. "I think that would be for the best."

They left the small room and wandered past the nurses' station onto the ward.

Sienna was sitting up in bed, cradling her newborn son. "Oh, you. What are you doing here?" The young mother's gaze drifted between Sara and Josie. "What's going on? Mum, have you been crying?" She gasped and placed a hand over her mouth then dropped it again. "It's not James, is it?"

"Let me have the baby, love, just for a minute." Josie relieved Sienna of the little bundle and sat in the chair next to her daughter's bed.

"Hello, Sienna. Congratulations, he looks a good weight," Sara said with a smile.

"Eight pounds ten. Please, tell me what you know, Inspector. Have you found him?"

"We have. I'm sorry…"

She didn't get any further. Sienna let out a piercing scream. The two nurses appeared at her bedside.

"What on earth is wrong?" the older one asked.

Tears streamed down Sienna's face. "He's dead. Is that what you're telling me?" she whispered as if saying it out loud would make the news seem more real, Sara presumed.

"Yes. I apologise for breaking the news to you while you're in hospital, but your mother and I agreed you should know as soon as possible."

"I can't believe it." She glanced at her new bundle of joy. "He'll never get to see him, to play with him, to love him. I think he would've been an excellent father. He told me he'd change when the baby was born."

Sara was quick to pounce on such a revelation, aware it would give her the opportunity to delve deeper into James's past. "Change? In what way, Sienna?"

She ran a hand over her face. It was then that Sara noticed the fading bruise on Sienna's forearm.

She clutched Sienna's arm and asked, "Did he do this to you? Did he abuse you, love?"

"Yes. He promised he'd change, swore to God he would, not that he believed in God."

*Run For Your Life*

The two nurses slipped back to their station now that things were calmer.

"Why put up with it, Sienna?" Sara asked.

"He loved me, in his own way. He wasn't always beating me up. The beatings had died down to only one or two a week."

Sara caught Josie shaking her head out of the corner of her eye, but her attention remained solely on Sienna. "Why? Did he say why he beat you?"

"He usually did it when I spoke out against him. Other times he was really loving and treated me like a princess. Usually that was in front of his friends. How did he die?"

"I have to tell you that James met a very gruesome end. I can't go into detail, but we believe he was murdered."

Fresh tears tumbled from her eyes. "Who would do such a thing? Did they know he was going to be a father any day?"

"I can't answer those questions, not yet, love. I need to ask you if you knew about James's past, or more to the point, what you knew about it."

Sienna's gaze lowered, and she wrung her hands in her lap but didn't reply.

"What do you know, Sienna?" Sara pushed.

"He told me about that night."

"The night of the rape? You were aware of that?"

"What the hell were you still doing with him, Sienna?" her mother said, shaking her head.

"Because I loved him, Mum."

"How could you love a rapist? Did he ever rape you, child?"

Sienna shook her head, but Sara was far from convinced by her response.

"Did he?" Sara asked.

"Once. It was my fault, I goaded him and pushed his buttons."

"Jesus, why? Why put up with something like that? No man is ever worth going through that for, love. I thought I brought you up with better morals than that," her mother said, her voice softening.

"Not now, Mum. Please, don't turn your back on me when I need you the most."

Josie laid a hand on her daughter's. "I would never do such a thing. I'm sorry, I shouldn't have blamed you. You were probably in a difficult position."

"I was. No one can help or understand when a woman is in that type of situation."

"Were you scared of him, Sienna?" Sara asked.

She nodded. "Yes, most of the time, now I think of it. But I had the hope to cling to, the promise that everything would change once the baby was born."

"You couldn't really believe that, Sienna?" her mother asked.

"I did. I know now how foolish that was of me. I would never have allowed him to have laid a hand on my child," she protested.

"And how many thousands of other women in abusive marriages have said the same thing over the years, do you reckon?" Josie shook her head.

"Pack it in, Mum. I don't need this, not now."

"Can I ask when he confided in you about the rape, Sienna?" Sara jumped in quickly before things escalated between mother and daughter.

"About two years ago. Oh God, there's something else you should know."

Sara frowned. "Go on."

"He was in court last year. A girl, a customer at the pub, said he touched her up. He got off with it in court. That's when the beatings started getting worse, when I gave him grief about it. That's when he raped me, as punishment." Her gaze drifted over to the baby. "Nine months ago or thereabouts, he's the result of that night."

"Oh my God, you poor, poor child. You should have told me. I would've supported you. I'd have also come round there and wiped the bloody floor with the bastard. He had no right treating you that way, sweetheart, no right."

"I didn't want to put you in that position, Mum. I thought I could handle it. I'm sorry. Please, don't think badly of me."

Sara's eyes pricked. It was such a touching scene between the two women, one far stronger than the other. "I'm sorry you were subjected to all of this, Sienna. Can you tell me if anyone has contacted James recently, you know, about the incident from five years ago?"

"I don't think so, no. You truly think his death is to do with what went on back then? Why? After all this time has elapsed? What about the girl? Have you spoken to her?"

"I don't know why. But yes, I've spoken to the girl, and my initial take on things is that she's not involved in the murders."

"Murders? What murders? I thought only James had been killed."

"There were five men that night, and three of them have been killed this week."

"No way! Then she has to be involved, doesn't she?"

"You'd think so, however, after questioning the young lady, I don't think she has it in her. She's still struggling with the trauma she went through that night."

"How dreadful, after five years?" Sienna said, shaking her head.

"I know rape is rape, but, I think it would likely affect people differently, given the circumstances in which the crime was committed."

"What do you mean by that?" Sienna asked.

"I'm no expert on the subject, but if someone is raped by a stranger or strangers, it would have far more impact on that person's mental state than when the rape takes place within a relationship." Sara waved a hand. "Oh, forget it. Saying it aloud just makes my assumptions sound ridiculous. At the end of the day, rape is rape, no matter what the circumstances are."

"No, I think you're probably right," Sienna agreed. "I pooh-poohed the incident quickly because I loved James, but I knew him. If he'd been a stranger, then yes, I'm sure I would've dealt with things very differently. So what happens now? Oh God, his parents need to know. I don't have to tell them, do I?"

"No. I can do it. Can you tell me where they live?"

"Miles away. Up in Cheshire somewhere. Mum, pass me my handbag, will you?"

Josie handed the child back to Sienna and opened the cupboard to remove her bag. "Shall I get your address book out?"

"No, I have their address on my phone."

Josie withdrew the phone, entered a password her daughter gave her and scrolled through the contacts for Karen and Denis Stanley's address and phone number. Sara jotted down the information and made a mental note to ring Cheshire police as soon as she got back to the station.

"Thanks for the information. Is there anything else you can think of that I should know?"

"I don't think so."

"His parents must be aware of the rape case, I take it?" Sara probed.

"Yes, he told me they employed an excellent barrister who got them all off. I suppose money talks. They're quite wealthy, you see."

"I'm with you. Thanks for the information, Sienna. One last thing and then I'll get out of your hair. Was James still in contact with the other gang members?"

"Yes, I think so. No, he definitely was. He quite often mentioned meeting them at the pub where he worked."

"I see. Okay, thanks for all your help. Congratulations on the birth of your son, and my condolences on your loss of James."

"Good riddance," Josie mumbled.

"Don't start, Mum," Sienna warned.

Josie folded her arms and huffed out a breath. "I'm entitled to my opinion. You'll soon come to realise what a waste of space he was, love."

"I doubt it, Mum. He will always be the father of my son."

Sara backed away. "I'll leave you to it. I'll be in touch as the investigation progresses, okay?"

"Thank you, Inspector, I'd appreciate that."

Sara smiled at both of the women and left the ward. On her way to the lift she rotated her shoulders in an attempt to relieve the tension that had surfaced during the conversation with Sienna. *Jesus, some people need a good shake if they can't see what's in front of them!*

## 10

Back at the station, she bumped into Luke Renshaw in the reception area. He smiled tautly and tried to swerve around her, but she was having none of it.

She placed a hand on his chest. "Hey, not trying to avoid me, are you, Luke?"

"No, nothing of the sort. I have to go. I'll catch up with you later."

"Wait. I need to know how the investigation is going."

"Later, Sara. I've warned you not to hassle me." He pushed through the exit and disappeared.

Sara shrugged at Jeff. "What did I say?"

"Sorry about that, ma'am. He should have taken time out to speak to you."

"Anyone would think he had something to hide."

"I don't think so. He's a bit flighty, that one, if you ask me."

"Keep your ear to the ground for me, Jeff."

He saluted her. "You can count on me."

"I know I can. See you later."

She plodded up the stairs to the incident room but changed her mind en route and ended up outside the DCI's office. "Is she available?" she asked Mary.

"I'll make sure, but yes, she's free as far as I know."

Mary opened the DCI's door and poked her head in. "DI Ramsey to see you, ma'am."

"Send her in, will you?"

Mary stood back, allowing Sara to squeeze past her.

"Thanks."

"Ah, Sara, come in, sit down. What can I do for you?"

"Morning, boss. I have a dilemma I need to run past you, if that's okay?"

"About your brother's death?"

Sara shook her head. "No, I've put that on hold for now. I just saw Renshaw, but he was in a rush and couldn't tell me anything. I don't suppose you've heard anything on that front, have you?"

"No. I can't say I have. Want me to chase him up for you?"

"Yes and no. Maybe it's too soon. No, leave it for now."

"Okay, let me know if you change your mind. What's up?"

Sara heaved out a sigh. "Well, it's the case or cases I'm working on. Something major has come to light, and I don't know what to do with the information. Can I run it past you, see what your take on it is?"

Carol Price sat back in her chair and intertwined her fingers over her stomach. "Go for it."

"Okay, I'm not sure if you're aware or not, but we're up to three murders. The pathologist believes they're all linked and so do I, given the other information we've uncovered about the victims."

"Do tell. I'm disappointed to hear we have yet another serial killer in our midst, though."

"Yeah, me, too. The three men all formed part of a gang who, five years ago, raped an eighteen-year-old girl."

"Whoa! Seriously? And you think she's the one bumping these fuckers...excuse me, these men off?"

"That's just it. Having spoken to the girl, who appears to still be struggling with her emotions and mental state, no, I don't think she could possibly be our perpetrator."

"Hmm...so, who is?"

Sara held her hands up in the air and let them drop onto her thighs. "At this point, we're not sure. The team are doing the background checks on the family now. The stepfather was none too pleased to see me and Carla last night when we showed up at their house, but I'm not sure if I'm guilty of reading too much into his obnoxious attitude or what?"

"It's not like you to have doubts, Sara."

"I know. Hands up, I don't think it's to do with Tim's death, but on the other hand, I'm not sure. I have confusion running through my veins right now, hence my coming to you, seeking advice."

"In regard to what?"

"Sorry, I'm going around the houses here. Here's the rub. Emma Wyatt, the girl who was raped, has a four-year-old daughter."

"Jesus! A consequence of the rape?"

"That's correct. My dilemma is, she knows who the father is. He's our first victim, Douglas Connor."

"I see. Did the man know about the child before his death?"

"No. I'm wondering if I should tell his parents or not. In my book, I believe they have a right to know, but would I be the right person to divulge such a secret after all these years? Would I be causing unnecessary problems? What if they decide to go for the child in a custody battle?"

"Is that likely? Has the mother mistreated the child?"

"No, not from what I could see, but she does have mental health problems that may go against her if they do. My head is caught up in a tornado on this one. How would you handle it if you were in my shoes?"

"I would feel obliged to tell them. It's their flesh and blood regardless of the circumstances, if the woman is adamant that he's the father."

"She is. She has no doubt about it. When I raised the subject with her, well, her stepfather went ballistic and virtually threw me out of the house for suggesting such a ridiculous notion, which is probably why I'm debating whether it's the right thing to do or not."

"He's just being overprotective. In his defence, I don't blame him.

However, it doesn't alter the fact that these poor people have a right to know if they have a grandchild out there. Do you know if they have others?"

"No, I don't. They seemed nice people when I had to break the news about their son's death the other day. I wouldn't feel right keeping the information from them."

"Then do it. If you receive any flak from either party refer them back to me and I'll deal with them, if that's what you want."

Sara smiled. "You'd do that?"

"Of course. I've always got your back, Sara, you should know that by now."

"I do. I'm so appreciative of your kindness."

"Phooey, kindness smindness, it's nothing of the sort. All I'm doing is covering my back. If you got fired, where the fuck would that leave me?"

Sara laughed. "Okay, I'll get the team organised and venture out to see them."

"You do that. How's the investigation going?"

"It's a tough one. Oh, while I'm here, I might as well ask you if you'd give the all-clear for some overtime."

"How come?"

"We've got two more gang members left. I think we should keep them under surveillance."

"You have my permission to go ahead. How long?"

"Exactly—for how long? That was going to be my next question."

"Well, knowing how tight we are on funds this quarter, my response would have to be no longer than a week. How's that?"

"That should take the pressure off us a little, boss. Thanks so much. I'd better crack on now. Lots to do, people to see et cetera."

"Keep me abreast of things, if you would. And Sara…"

Sara reached for the handle of the door and turned when the chief called her name. "Yes, boss?"

"Stop frigging doubting yourself and your abilities. I know you're going through personal shit right now, but give yourself a break now and again, right? Use your team, they're the best we have around here."

"Thanks, boss, I will. And yes, you're right, they're the bestest around." Sara grinned.

"Go catch me another serial killer. That's an order."

"I'll try my hardest."

Sara left the office and made her way back to the incident room. She found the team hard at work. She clapped to draw everyone's attention and disclosed everything she knew about James Stanley that Sienna had conveyed at the hospital.

"What the fuck!" Carla said, throwing a pen across the desk. "Why do women put up with shits like that? Want me to check the files, see what I can find about the other case?"

"Yep, do that. I've also been to see the DCI. She's agreed with me in regard to informing the Connors they have a granddaughter. Carla, you and I should take a ride out there soon."

Carla pulled a face. "I still think it's the wrong thing to do."

"I hear you. I wouldn't feel right keeping that type of information to myself, though. First, I need to ring Cheshire police, get someone to pay James's family a visit. I don't trust myself to speak to them over the phone, knowing his bloody record and the fact they've bailed him out of trouble a couple of times over the years. Makes my blood boil thinking about it."

She hurriedly made the call. The desk sergeant at the other end promised to send a higher-ranking officer out to break the news which Sara shared with him over the phone. He promised to get back to her if there was an ounce of trouble from them.

Sara ended the call. *Thanks, I can do without any more trouble landing on my doorstep.*

She returned to the incident room where she organised the team. "Listen up, folks, the chief has given us the go-ahead to carry out surveillance or babysit the other two men. I know that's going to stick in all of our throats, but our main role is to protect and serve the public, so that's what we're going to do."

A few groans and mutterings floated back to her.

"Carla and I will take our turn out there, don't worry. When I get the chance, I will call on Thornton and Iverson, make them aware of the situation, but I have another pressing engagement to attend to. So, Craig and Will, you take Iverson, and Barry and…let's see, Marissa, are you up for tagging along with Barry on this one?"

"I'd love to, as long as he doesn't insist on stuffing burgers down his neck and gassing me out every five minutes."

Barry stared at her open-mouthed, tutted and said, "Would I? I think you're getting me mixed up with young Craig over there."

"Oi, you!" Craig shouted.

Sara clapped, snapping them out of the frivolity. "Okay, guys, enough. Let's get the show on the road. Report back to me when you're in situ. Familiarise yourselves with both men's homes, work addresses and vehicles before you go, just in case either one of them is not at home." She glanced up at the clock—it was almost midday. "In your shoes, I'd opt for the work address first. Okay?"

The four officers nodded their acceptance.

"Right, Jill and Christine, in our absence if you can dig deep into Emma's and her family's background, maybe pull up the archives of what went on during the court case as well, that would be great."

Both women nodded and got back to their computers.

"Are you ready, Carla?"

Her partner groaned and gave a reluctant nod. "As I'll ever be. Have you rung them, to make sure they're at home?"

"We'll do it on the way. Come on, time's not on our side on this one. The sooner we get out there the sooner we can get on with the investigation."

As it happened, both Douglas Connor's parents were at home when they arrived.

"Hello, there," Mrs Connor said, smiling cautiously when she greeted them at the door. "Do you have some news for us?"

*Run For Your Life*

She gestured for them to come in out of the drizzle which had followed them out of town.

"Thanks. In a manner of speaking, yes," Sara said.

"Go through to the lounge. Lee's in there. We're going through the funeral arrangements." Sadness clouded her face, and her shoulders sagged. She expelled a large breath and stood upright again before they walked into the lounge.

Sara presumed her husband would have had a pop at her if she'd shed any more tears.

"Lee, this is DI Ramsey and her partner—sorry, dear, I've forgotten your name," she said to Carla.

"It's DS Jameson, but it really doesn't matter."

"Pleased to meet you. Take a seat. Barbara, I'm sure the ladies would like a cuppa."

Sara held up a hand. "We've not long had one back at the station, so we'll decline this time round. Thanks all the same."

Sara and Carla sat on the couch opposite the married couple.

"Fair enough. What's this all about? Have you caught the bastard who did this to Douglas?" Lee was quick to ask.

"I'm sorry, not yet, but we're closing in on them." Sara sucked in a deep breath and then continued. "However, I do have some news that I believe you should be made aware of."

The couple glanced at each other, gripped each other's hand and then faced Sara again.

"Go on," Lee prompted.

"This is extremely difficult for me to say, so please bear with me."

"Oh dear! You're worrying me now," Barbara said, her voice weak as if she was choked up with unshed tears.

"Please, don't worry. Right, I need to go back five years, to the court case. Do you remember that?"

The couple's grasp on each other's hand tightened.

"Of course we do. It's blighted our lives ever since. What does this have to do with our son's death?" Lee demanded.

"I believe, indirectly, a great deal. That's the angle we're going on anyway. The thing is, this week, three members of the gang involved in that incident have been murdered."

"What? Are you winding us up?" Lee jumped to his feet and paced.

"Now, Lee, calm down, you're not going to do your blood pressure any good ranting and raving about things. Sit down," Barbara insisted.

Her husband threw himself onto the couch again and reached for his wife's hand.

"That was the vilest day of our lives, well, not a day as such, that whole period. From the day he was arrested up until the court case. You know, it ruined our relationship," Lee confessed.

"In what way?" Sara asked quietly, doing her best to keep things calm.

"We knew he was guilty but we did what any other parent would have done in our position, we backed our son to the hilt. You know, five years later we're still paying off the exorbitant loan we took out for the barrister's fees. The other boys' parents were well off compared to us. Barbara and I have always had to graft hard for any money coming into this house."

"I had no idea, I'm sorry to hear that. I have to ask, why didn't you accept his guilt for what it was?"

"Would you? If he was your child? You do anything and everything in your power to keep your child safe and out of harm's way," Barbara said, a sob escaping soon after.

Lee wrapped an arm around her shoulder and pulled her close. "Don't go getting yourself upset again, love."

"It's hard not to, I miss him so much. He had his faults, I know that, but you accept bad faults when they're your own flesh and blood."

"Hush now." Lee rocked her.

Sara's throat clogged up. She coughed to clear the blockage. "Oh dear, well, I have some news that I'm not sure how you're going to take or be able to process. I have to tell you that I sought advice from my immediate superior because I just wasn't sure if you should be told or not."

*Run For Your Life*

"My God, whatever are you going to tell us?" Barbara wiped her nose on a tissue and stared at Sara.

"Well, sometime after the court case, the young woman who your son was guilty of raping, as you've just confirmed, had a baby."

"No! Oh my, that poor girl. Dear Lord, fancy that. Oh gosh, what absolute torture she must have gone through, and all the time she knew she was pregnant."

"Ssh now, love. Let the inspector finish what she has to say," Lee said.

"It's such a hard one to call, considering what this young lady has gone through over the years, especially as the truth has now come out that you believe your son was guilty. Can you imagine the pain and mental torture Emma has had to contend with for five long years?" Sara bit down on her tongue, her own feelings clearly making their mark during her speech.

"There's no need to rub it in, we're aware how wrong we were to back him. You have to look at it from our situation. The others all put in a *not guilty* plea and the parents fronted up with the money. We had to conform, we had no choice, no matter how much it grieved us to do that. I swear, I gave my lad the hiding of his life the night he admitted his guilt to us. I'll always feel guilty about that, but Barbara and I are proud, honest people. To be confronted with that sort of behaviour from our lad, well, there's no way I was going to put up with it, I can tell you. I wanted to kick him out, but Barbara talked me out of it. Every time I looked at him, all I saw was a vile excuse for a man."

"Lee…how can you say that? Speak ill of the dead?" his wife chastised him.

"Easily, love. That one night split this family apart, you have to admit that. It's the reason I took on the extra work and decided to start volunteering to do the jobs abroad because I couldn't stand being around my own son, knowing that he was a fucking rapist." Tears glistened in his eyes. He pulled away from his wife and shoved his hands between his legs.

Barbara shook her head. "Why didn't you say something? You've kept it bottled up all these years, love?"

"What could I say? You could see no wrong in what he'd done."

"That's not true, Lee. I loved the very bones of that boy but still didn't like him some days. My heart went out to the girl. I contemplated getting in touch with her a few times, just to check on how she was doing, but figured if I did that, all it would be doing was showing her that Douglas was guilty of the sin he'd committed. I was in a terrible dilemma, one that has eaten away at me for some time, and now you're telling us she has a child. Dare I ask who the father is? If…they all, umm…took their turn with her that night, how would you be able to tell who the real father is? Or am I being naïve?"

"Yes, as usual, Barbara. It only takes one sperm to fertilise a damn egg, or are you forgetting the basics of biology?"

"There's no need for that tone of voice, Lee. My head is swimming with funeral details as well, you know. Give me some slack, please?"

"I'm sorry, that outburst was uncalled for." Lee faced Sara again. "So, why are you here? The *real* reason?"

His eyes narrowed, and Sara got the impression he knew full well the reason behind their visit.

"We've yet to confirm it, but Emma is confident she knows who the father is."

"Who?" Barbara asked breathlessly, grabbing her husband's arm.

Sara nodded. "I think you've guessed. I've seen, we've seen, the child and I believe she is the spitting image of your son."

Barbara and Lee froze for a few seconds, their mouths gaping open at the news. Barbara ended the silence by breaking down in tears. Lee had the decency, despite having a go at her moments earlier, to throw an arm around her shoulder and hug her tightly, soothing her gently.

"I'm sorry if this has come as a shock. I needed to let you know. I'm not sure what you can do about it, given the circumstances. Maybe you should have a word with your solicitor about what legal rights you have for visiting the child in the future once a DNA test has been done."

"Ha! More bloody costs to consider. No wonder you never see a poor solicitor or barrister walking around town."

Barbara perked up at the news. "It doesn't matter about the cost, she might be our flesh and blood, and we're entitled to see her."

Sara held up a hand. "Seriously, Barbara, I think you need to tread carefully. Emma is quite within her rights to prevent any form of access, you know, after how the child was conceived. You really need to take that on board."

"Oh, I will. But no one is going to stop me from seeing or being a part of that child's life if she's part of our family."

"Have you listened to yourself?" Lee swivelled in his seat and grasped her hands in his. "You need to prepare yourself for rejection. If the child's mother doesn't want to know, then we have to listen to her needs and ignore our own. Don't go blowing this up out of all proportion, love. Let the consequences sink in for now."

"She may be our grandchild, I refuse to dismiss that fact. After Douglas's death, I need something to cling on to. Don't deny me that, Lee, please, don't do that."

Lee's head snapped around to face Sara and Carla again. "Wait just a minute, it's all starting to slot together now."

Sara cringed inwardly but kept her poker face intact and tilted her head. "Sorry, I'm not with you."

"You came in here and told us that three of the five men had been murdered this week. Are you telling us you think she's killed them?"

"No, I'm not saying that at all. She's very timid, is afraid to go out on her own. Only ever goes out to take her daughter to playschool, in fact. There's no way she'd be in the frame for killing the men."

"Okay, if not her, what about another member of her family? Come on, do I have to do the detective work for you? For God's sake, it's all making sense to me. It has to be one of her family, it has to be, or someone she knows perhaps," Lee added as an afterthought.

"Hold on a minute, let's not go getting ahead of ourselves here. My team are doing the necessary background checks on the family now. Hopefully something will show up there. Around the time of the court case, did you have anything to do with them?"

Lee shook his head. "No. They showed up in force every day to support her. You know, the father, mother and the brother."

Sara raised a hand. "Wait, a brother? We haven't stumbled across him yet. What can you tell me about him?"

He shrugged. "Not much. He was always by the girl's side. Seemed a bit of a wimp to me. Quite tall but very skinny. He refused to look any of us in the eye. I suppose, thinking back, that was understandable."

"I see. Well, thanks for the information. Did anyone else show up at court, another friend or family member perhaps?"

The couple glanced at each other and then shook their heads.

"No, I don't think so," Lee finally said. "You need to do those checks quickly, before whoever is doing this goes after the rest of them."

"Don't worry, it's all in hand. We're on our way to see the other two members of the gang after we've finished here. Are you both going to be all right?"

"Yes, we'll cope," Lee assured her. "Is that all?"

"Yes, for now. We'll be in touch soon, I hope. Please, my advice would be to let what I've told you sink in for a few days before you seek help from your solicitor. You know the costs involved. Don't go getting into further debt." She stood, and Carla followed her out into the hallway.

"Thank you for sharing the news with us today." Lee passed them and held the door open.

"You're welcome. Take care of each other. Maybe let things settle down for now and reassess after the funeral."

"Good thinking. We'll do that. Do your best for us, won't you?"

"You have my word on that, Mr Connor."

Sara and Carla jumped back in the car.

Sara drove away from the house, then indicated and pulled into the kerb a few streets later. "I'm going to contact the station. We need to find out more about this brother. He's news to us."

She punched in the number of the station and was patched through to her team. Christine took the call.

"Hi, it's me, how are things going there?"

"Hi, boss, you must have a sixth sense or something, I was just about to call you."

Sara put the phone on speaker. "Oh, about what?"

"I might have discovered something relevant and wanted to run it past you."

"Go on, Christine."

"I did as you requested and searched through the archives around the court case and discovered Emma has a stepbrother called Teddy Masterton. We're not aware of him, are we? If we are, I must've missed it during our briefings."

"No, we weren't aware. Hey, by coincidence, I was calling you to see what you could find on him as the Connors have just mentioned him when we broke the news to them."

"Cool. How did it go?"

"As expected. I think I blew their minds with the bloody news. Back to Teddy, what do we know about him?"

"He lives at the same house with Emma and her parents."

"Hmm...that's strange, he wasn't there the other night."

"Maybe he was otherwise engaged, holding James Stanley captive," Carla piped up.

Sara held her hand up for Carla to fist bump it. "Carla could have a point. Okay, let's see what car he drives and what job he does and go from there. Carla and I are going to pay the other two gents a visit. I'll check in with the surveillance teams first. I have a good feeling about this one now, ladies. Let's hit it hard and fast."

"Will do, boss. I'll get digging now."

Sara ended the call and then rang the two teams out on the road. "Craig, it's me. Anything to report?"

"We're outside the factory where Brad Iverson works. His car is here, and I've checked inside, and yes, he's here."

"Okay, give me the location, and we'll shoot over there to see him."

Craig gave her the name of the factory and the postcode, which Carla jotted down, then she hung up and rang Marissa.

"Hey you, it's me. Any news?"

"We're outside B&Q. I nipped inside and checked if Aaron is at work. He is."

"Okay, we're going over to see Iverson first and then we'll swing by and have a chat with Thornton. Hang tight for a while, we'll see you soon."

"Rightio, boss."

## 11

Sara knew she shouldn't, but she hated Brad Iverson on sight. He was handsome, the type who revelled in it, aware of all the admiring glances he was attracting from the ladies in the surrounding area. The receptionist at the factory had requested Sara and Carla take a seat while she tried to contact Iverson. It was despatch day, she'd told them, all hands were needed to ensure the lorries got away on time.

However, when Iverson showed up a few minutes after being summoned, Sara got the impression he hadn't had a stressful day in his life.

"Police, you say? Have I done something wrong?" He smiled.

Sara couldn't help but wonder how many hearts he'd broken over the years with that devastating, killer smile. It had little to no effect on her, though, she made sure of that.

"You police officers get prettier by the day. Female coppers used to be so much butcher in the old days."

"Back when you were arrested, five years ago, you mean?" Sara aimed her retort and got a direct hit.

His eyes narrowed. He glanced over his shoulder to see if the receptionist had heard. She had and was staring at Iverson, her eyes wide with a mixture of shock and curiosity.

He turned back to Sara and hissed, "Keep your voice down, no one knows about that around here."

"Tut tut, shouldn't you have declared that on your CV, Mr Iverson?"

His eyes narrowed further into tiny slits. "No. In case you've forgotten, I was found *not* guilty of the preposterous offence."

Sara smiled and nodded. "Officially, you were indeed. Tell me, do you sleep well at night, knowing that you gang raped that woman and then called her an outright liar in court?"

He walked to the other side of the large reception area, expecting them to follow him.

Sara and Carla were happy to oblige.

"Why? Why are you here making these accusations now, after all these years?"

"Accusations? I wouldn't call what I said that, it's a fact. We've got it on good authority that you and the other men involved in that heinous crime lied through your teeth to the jury."

"What of it?" he snarled and then paced the area, clearly shaken by having the past dredged up.

"Are you still in contact with the other men?"

"Yes, now and again, why?" he bit back.

"Are you aware that three of them have been killed this week?"

"What?" he screeched, running a hand through his short black hair, spoiling his neatly moussed style.

"Now are you going to listen to me and stop playing the big I am?"

"I suppose. Who's dead?"

"Douglas, Wesley and James."

"Shit! Shit! Shit! What the fuck are you doing about it?"

"Our job. We're investigating all three crimes and have come to the conclusion that the same perpetrator is involved."

"Fuck! Really? Is that it? I would've thought it would've been blatantly obvious. You don't have to be Einstein to know what's going on, or am I reading things into it?"

"Like I say, we're on the case."

"So, why are you here? Do you know something, something about me?"

"Apart from the fact you got off in court for the detestable crime you committed, we're here to warn you to be vigilant."

"What? Oh yeah, and I can do without your sarcastic references to the past. Did the other guys get warned before they were bumped off? Shit, I can't believe they're gone. We've been friends since primary school. Stuck together through thick and thin."

"And through a shambolic court case where you went out of your way to lie together, too, right?" There was no way Sara was going to sit back and let this guy get away with what he did and the ruddy trouble it had caused.

"Bollocks! That's not the problem now, you catching the sick shit going around killing my pals is the frigging problem. You need to toodle back to your car and get out there, to search for this fucking bastard."

Sara raised a hand. "And you need to stop issuing orders and open your ears. We're here to advise you to remain vigilant at all times until the culprit is apprehended."

"I heard you the first time. I'll do what's necessary as long as you tell me you're doing the same. Now get out of my hair, I have work to do."

He stormed away and took his frustration out on the door behind him. A scream sounded on the other side. He glanced back over his shoulder while he helped the woman he'd knocked over to her feet. Sara smiled smugly at him.

"Come on, it's pointless us being here. Let him get what's coming to him," Sara grumbled.

Outside by the car, Carla said, "I can't believe you said that!"

"What?"

"About him getting what's coming to him. What's wrong with you, Sara?"

"Wrong with me? Nothing, as far as I know. You heard him, he's a conceited ratbag, and that's me putting things mildly. There are far worse names I could use for the moron. If he wants to dismiss what I tell him about being vigilant then that's his lookout, not mine. Prick!"

Carla shook her head in disgust and slipped into the passenger seat.

Sara sucked in a few deep breaths to calm herself before she got in the car. *Why did I allow him to wind me up back there? Because he's a cretin and a rapist!* She had seen the way he'd looked her up and down. He'd tainted her, leaving her feeling as though a million cockroaches were burrowing their way deep into her skin. She detested men who had the ability to do that to a woman. Not for the first time she found herself thanking her lucky stars she had a decent man like Mark to share her home with.

Silence filled the car during the drive to B&Q. She and Carla waved at Marissa and Barry and headed inside to speak to Aaron Thornton. Sara braced herself for more of the same attitude. She was wrong. When Aaron stopped at the customer service desk, outwardly he appeared to be the complete opposite of the jumped-up shit they'd just had the pleasure of dealing with.

"Hi, Aaron, is there somewhere private where we can have a chat?"

He frowned. "Have I done something wrong?"

"Not really." Sara smiled and inclined her head. "Time is against us, so the quicker the better, if you don't mind."

"Sorry. Yes, okay." He started off in one direction and changed his mind.

"Calm down," Sara whispered.

"Sorry, yes, okay, I'll do that. Sonia, is the office free?" he asked the girl at the till.

"Yep, it should be. I'll be manning the desk for a while. Go ahead and use it," she replied, her gaze shifting between the three of them.

Sara and Carla followed the anxious young man into the square office.

He motioned for them to take a seat and chose to sit on the edge of the desk in front of them. "What's this about?"

Sara smiled and scratched the side of her head. "Okay, this isn't easy for me to say, so bear with me a second. There's no need for you to get worked up, though."

*Run For Your Life*

"I'll be the judge of that. What brings the police to my workplace? I haven't done anything wrong." He gasped. "Damn, nothing's happened to Mum, has it?"

"No, it's nothing like that. I promise."

"What is it then?" he asked, clearly confused.

"It's regarding something that happened five years ago, Aaron. Is it all right if I call you Aaron?"

"Of course. Oh God, I know what you're talking about. What about it?" he asked, his voice trailing off.

"We're aware of what you did back then and that the courts found you not guilty, however, what I'm about to tell you might come as a shock to you."

"What are you saying? We were innocent, me and the other lads."

"Whether you were innocent or not, there have been three major crimes that have taken place this week in connection with that crime."

"Sorry, could you say that a bit clearer?"

"I apologise. Okay, I was trying to soften the blow and messed up. This week, three members of your gang have ended up in the mortuary."

His head jutted forward on his skinny neck. "What? You must be mistaken. This can't be right. Dead, is that what you're telling me?"

"Yes, Douglas, Wesley and James have all been murdered. We believe their deaths are a direct result of the rape the five of you committed five years ago."

"How? Uhh…rape, it wasn't rape, the courts found us not guilty. We didn't do anything to that girl." His gaze drifted off to the left, a clear indication that he was lying.

"Please, don't take us for fools, Aaron. We have recently spoken to witnesses who confirmed you were all guilty of raping Emma Wyatt. Anyway, we're here to warn you to remain vigilant."

"Why? Oh fuck! You think this madman is going to come after me next, is that what you're telling me?"

"Possibly. Maybe not. All I'm saying is that until we have the culprit in custody, I think you should be aware that you might be on someone's radar. I'd hate to think of you joining your friends."

"Bloody hell! Why? After all these years. I never wanted to get involved, you know. Brad forced me to do it."

"The fact is that you were there and very much involved. Someone obviously has a grudge against all of you and is dishing out their own form of justice."

"Can't you do something to help me? Put me in a police protection scheme?"

"It's not as simple as that. We're doing our best to catch the culprit which is proving difficult as we're unsure who the perpetrator is yet."

"It seems to me like it could be the girl we did it to, or am I wrong in thinking that?"

"We've questioned her, and sorry, but we believe she's innocent. She barely leaves the house and only cares for her daughter."

"Daughter? There you go, if she's married, what about her partner then? Go after him."

"She doesn't have a partner. The child was an unfortunate consequence which came from that night, you see, that's how we know none of you were innocent."

"Damn! That poor girl. I tried my best not to get involved. Brad, well, he told me to man up or get kicked out of the gang. I was young, I didn't know any better back then."

"Are you trying to tell me that you believed raping a girl was okay and normal behaviour for a group of young men?"

"Yes and no. Peer pressure, you have no idea how demeaning that is. I had to do it. If I hadn't, he would have kicked me out of the gang, and it wouldn't have ended there either."

"Meaning what?"

He sighed. "Brad has a lot of influence in Hereford. If you speak out against him, well, the writing would be on the wall for you. Let's just say I wouldn't have been here today, if I'd spoken out."

"So, let me see if I'm understanding you properly here. You were watching your own back while you raped an innocent girl. Probably put her through torturous hours of pain, shame and misery, is that your take?"

"If you put it like that, then yes, I was in the wrong. I know that now. I was young and easily influenced in those days. If I could take it all back, I would, in a heartbeat. But what's done is done. People need to get on with their lives, not take umbrage years later and start killing off those who were responsible. She's obviously to blame, she has to be. It's her you should be reading the riot act to, not me."

"I was doing no such thing. Aaron, we're here to ensure you take this seriously and do all you can to keep yourself safe while we try and hunt this person down." Sara winced when she mentioned the word 'hunt'.

"I get that. Okay, is that it? Can I get back to work now?"

Sara shrugged. "If that's what you want?"

"I do. I need to be by myself to grieve the loss of my friends."

"Very well. Here's a card. Ring me if you need to speak to me about anything, okay?"

He took the card and stood. "Thanks."

They went their separate ways when they left the office. Sara noted the downward turn in the man's shoulders as he walked away from them.

"What did you make of him?" Carla asked on the way back to the car.

"I couldn't tell. One minute I thought he was remorseful, the next, I swear I detected a note of arrogance to his tone. Who the hell knows with these men? I'll just have a quick word with Marissa and Barry, I won't be long." She marched across the car park and jumped into the back seat of Marissa's vehicle. She apprised them of the situation and told them to remain there all day if necessary.

"Want us to follow him home, boss?" Barry asked, his gaze still trained on the main entrance.

"Yep, see him home and leave it an hour then call it a day, if you would. Carla and I are going back to the station. We found out that Emma has a brother who we didn't know about."

"Hmm...sounds promising," Marissa agreed.

"Keep in touch throughout the day. If he leaves the store, I want to hear about it, okay? And keep an eye on the vehicles coming and going during your time here, just in case the killer shows up."

Barry turned to look at her. "Have you seen how many cars come in and out of here during opening hours?"

She patted him on the shoulder and opened the back door. "I can imagine. Be good. There's a burger wagon around the corner, so you're in luck there."

"Thank God," Barry mumbled.

Sara strode back to the car, her mind full of 'what-if' scenarios which distracted her until the blast of a horn broke her out of her reverie.

"Stupid bitch. Fancy daydreaming in a busy car park," an irate man shouted out of his car window. He drew to a halt alongside her.

She glared at him and reached into her pocket for her warrant card. She shoved the ID in his face. "You want to say that again?" she dared him.

"Ugh…damn, sorry, I didn't mean any offence."

"Yeah, until the next time. Move on and keep your anger under control, and remember you're driving around a five-mile-an-hour car park, right?"

"Yeah, okay. I'll do that."

She shook her head and watched the man drive away and took note of his licence number, just in case. Men like him ticked her off. He probably had a small dick and was trying to make up for his lack of manhood by opening his big mouth and choosing to pick on who he perceived to be a dumb woman.

"Problems?" Carla asked.

She slipped into her seat. "Nothing I couldn't handle. Let's get back to the station, I'm in dire need of a caffeine fix."

At the station, Sara and Carla were on their way up the stairs to the incident room. She glanced up to make sure the way was clear only to see Luke Renshaw coming towards her.

She deliberately moved over, blocking his path. "Got time for a brief chat, Luke?"

"Not really, Sara. I've told you, let me handle this case. I'll update you when I have some news I deem worth sharing."

She folded her arms and tapped her foot halfway up the stairs. "Come on, we're talking about my brother here. Put yourself in my shoes for a moment, Luke. You'd want to know, wouldn't you?"

"Jesus. Yes, I would. You win. Not here, though, in your office."

The three of them raced up the stairs and into the incident room. Carla headed towards the coffee machine to do the honours while Sara ushered Luke into her office and closed the door. She rushed around her desk and threw herself into her chair.

"Go on. Tell me, and please, don't hold back. I've had a few days to come to terms with Tim's death, grant me with some sense."

"Okay. How much do you know about your brother?"

Her brow creased into a painful frown. "Meaning what?"

Carla entered the office, deposited two cups of coffee on the desk and then left.

"Meaning, how much did you know about your brother? It's a simple question, Sara."

"I heard you, I just didn't understand the question. Shit! You're worrying me now. What have you discovered about him?" She braced herself, clinging to the edge of the desk with her sweaty hands.

"He owed money, were you aware of that?"

"How much are we talking about?"

"A lot."

"Come on. How much?"

"Over a hundred grand."

Sara's tense shoulders sagged, and she slumped back in her chair. "What? To whom?"

"A loan shark. Actually, two of them. They're mean bastards."

"What are you telling me? You think they killed him?"

"Yep. Did you know he was a user, too?"

Sara nodded, slowly. "Lorraine pointed out the marks on his arms. Before that, I had no idea. I knew he was an alcoholic, I presumed that had killed him. What am I saying? No, I didn't, his throat was cut.

Ignore me, this has all come as a huge shock to me. Fuck! How am I going to tell my parents?"

He shrugged. "I'm sorry to break the news like this but, in my defence, you pushed me into a corner."

"It's okay. I don't blame you. Putting yourself in my shoes, you'd have done the same thing, wouldn't you?" She attempted a weak smile.

"Yep, you're probably right. Listen, I need to get on. My team and I are closing in on the loan sharks. They're both under surveillance, and we're hoping to nab them today."

Sara sat upright, the shock making way for her enthusiasm to catch the person responsible for Tim's death. "Go. Will you promise to keep me updated?"

"Of course. Don't worry, we'll get the fuckers, you have my word. Both men have been on our radar for years. Hopefully we can get the two gits off the streets soon, even if I have to make out they were working together on this one."

"Hang on, I wouldn't want you to do anything to jeopardise the case."

"It won't. Trust me." With that, Luke left her office.

Carla barged in a few seconds later. "Everything all right?"

Sara shook her head, still dazed by the news. "No, not really. My brother owed a ton of money to loan sharks and he was a junkie, apparently."

"What?" Carla shrieked. She looked behind her at the rest of the team, stepped into the room and flopped back against the closed door. "Shit! Define *a ton of money*. We knew about the drugs, right?"

"Over a hundred grand. Two loan sharks were after his blood. They succeeded in their mission."

"Holy crap! And you had no inclination about this at all?"

"No. I thought he had a drink problem, nothing major. Well, I say that, it was bad enough to break up his marriage, but you know what I mean. Bugger! I can't help feeling guilty, I let him down when he needed me the most."

"Sara, you're not to blame for this, none of you are. Your brother had his own life to lead and screw up. His death shouldn't haunt you for failing him. This was not your fault, you hear me?"

"I hear you. Try telling my parents that. Hell, how am I going to tell them this? It could bloody kill them."

"Can you leave things as they are for now, disguise the truth or withhold it from them until the case is over? I would."

"I think that's what I'll have to do. I'm going to feel awful doing it but I think it will be for the best. Sorry to put all this on you."

Carla waved the suggestion away. "Don't be. I'm your friend as well as your partner. Blimey! You've listened to me venting enough about Gary over the past few months. Treat this as payback."

"You're a good friend, Carla. Right, let's try and set this aside for now. We have a killer of our own to track down."

Carla nodded and left the room.

Sara was still contemplating her brother's death when the phone interrupted her. "DI Ramsey. How can I help?"

"She's gone!" someone screamed down the phone.

"Excuse me? Who is this?"

"My daughter…she's gone, and it's all your fault."

Sara recognised the voice now, and her heart dropped to her stomach. "Emma, is that you?"

"Yes…my daughter, you have to get her back."

"Where is she? You're not making any sense. Has someone taken her?"

"Yes, because you told them. You're to blame. I want her back. They have no right to take her. She's mine. She's all I have. She's my world. Help me!"

Sara's eyes pricked, and she swallowed down the bile in her throat. *What have I done?* "Emma, I'm coming to see you. Are you at home?"

"Yes, but that's only wasting time. I want my daughter back."

"Okay. Calm down. Can you tell me what happened?"

"I went to fetch her from school. We were close to home when a lorry pulled up alongside us. A man and a woman got out. I didn't think anything more about it, and then someone bashed me over the head. I woke up surrounded by the other mothers from school. They told me the elderly couple took my daughter. Tia was screaming. They all saw what happened and did nothing to help. She's gone. I want her back. Do something."

"Okay, Emma, I need you to try and remain calm. I'll sort this, don't worry. Stay at home. I'll be in touch soon. I'm so sorry this has happened. I'll make things right, I promise you."

"Hurry up. What if they hurt her? She'll be scared. I hate the thought of my baby being frightened and me not being there to comfort her." Emma's voice was strained and full of stress.

"I'll get back to you as soon as I can. Stay positive, Emma. If it's who I think it is, they won't hurt her."

"I hope not. I'll hold you responsible if they do." Emma slammed down the phone.

*Could this day possibly get any worse?* Sara got her shit together, left her desk and flew into the incident room. "Ladies, I need you to drop everything you're working on for now, we have an emergency situation that needs sorting ASAP."

"What's that?" Carla asked.

"I believe Emma Wyatt's daughter has been kidnapped by the Connors."

"Are you serious?" Carla shouted.

"Deadly. She was knocked out by a couple driving a lorry when she picked her daughter up from school. They're the only people I can think of who would risk doing such a terrible thing. We need to find them, and quickly. Shit, we're understaffed. Do I take the risk and call the others back to help or do we plough on ahead ourselves?" The uncertainty lay heavily on her shoulders.

"We've got this. There are four of us here. We can do this, boss," Carla confirmed with a smile.

"Okay. I'm sorry, my head is a mess right now. You're going to have to be my wingman on this, Carla, take up the slack if you think I'm doing things wrong."

Carla puffed out her cheeks. "Shit! No pressure there then. We've got this, as a team, we've got it."

"Right, Jill, can you sort out the CCTV in the area of the school?

I'm taking a punt there isn't any as it's way out in the sticks. Give it a try anyway."

"On it, boss."

"Christine, I need you to find out who Lee Connor drives for. Carla, you and I will start the background checks on the family. Who Barbara works for and if there are any other relatives or likely places they could have gone to."

"It's going to take us hours, but we can do this."

"I hope so. Shit, what if the killer finds out?"

"We can't think along those lines right now. Let's stick to the facts, what we know, and worry about the other details further down the line."

Sara nodded. "You're right. However, we need to be aware of the time factor involved and that the killer might be forced to do something drastic, if he or she is known to Emma." She pulled her hair from the roots. "Jesus, there's a mammoth task ahead of us."

Carla placed a hand on her arm. "We've got this, Sara. Stay focused and on track."

"I'm trying. Let's hit all this hard and fast, but thoroughly, ladies, no shortcuts, okay?"

The three other officers gave her the thumbs-up, and Sara let out a relieved sigh.

Two hours later, and they reflected on what they'd uncovered so far. The lorry had been picked up on the ANPR cameras heading north on the M5 and then taking the M6 motorway. Sara had managed to track down the Connors' daughter, Donna Watson. She'd been mortified by her parents' behaviour and promised to help the police in any way possible. She had confided that they had a second home up in the Lake District, on the edge of the national park; she felt that's where her parents would be heading.

Sara thanked the woman and pleaded with her not to make contact with her parents. Donna had agreed, wanting her parents home safely. She also begged Sara to go easy on them as her brother's murder had obviously hit them harder than any of them had realised.

Sara immediately called the local police, made them aware of the situation. She was passed on to an Inspector Kiltie who promised to deal with the problem himself and said he would get back to her as soon as the child was safe.

Later that afternoon, Sara had the beginnings of a headache brewing. Now that things had calmed down and a plan to rescue the child was in place, she congratulated her team and drifted back into her office. She popped a couple of Nurofen with a glass of water and, from her seat, looked up at the thunderous sky which appeared to match the day she was having. What a bloody day it had been, and it wasn't over yet. She picked up the phone and rang Mark.

"Hi, how are you?"

"Up to my neck in things here. Is it important, Sara? I don't wish to appear rude but, if I want to get home tonight, I need to crack on with things."

"Go. It's fine. I'll see you later. I might be late, that's all. Love you."

"I love you, too. Are you sure things are okay?"

"Fine. Bye, sweetheart." She ended the call and had only just popped the phone back in its docking station when it rang. "DI Sara Ramsey. How can I help?"

"It's DI Kiltie. Just calling you to let you know we have the child. She's safe and well, and the Connors are ashamed of what they've done. How do you want us to proceed?"

"Can you get the child back to me tonight? The mother is obviously eager to have her home."

"Of course. I'll get the transportation sorted ASAP. What about the Connors?"

"In the circumstances, can you go easy on them? I know that's asking a lot, but their grieving has played an enormous part in their decision-making."

"I can't just let them go with a slap on the wrist, if that's what you're asking."

"I know you can't, and I wouldn't expect that. I'll leave it up to you. My main concern is the safety of the child."

"She's fine. I'll get a couple of female officers to drive her back home tonight. Well, it'll probably be the early hours of the morning by the time they reach your neck of the woods."

"Thanks. I'll let the mother know you've found her and to expect her daughter home later. I can't thank you enough for this, Inspector."

"It's my pleasure. All in a day's work as they say. Thankfully, nothing bad happened on this occasion, always good to hear."

"So pleased about that. Thanks, Inspector." She ended the call and immediately rang Emma Wyatt.

Ben Masterton answered the call. "Have you found her?" he demanded abruptly.

"Is Emma there, sir?"

"She's standing beside me. I have you on speaker."

"Emma, are you there?"

"Yes, I'm here. Is Tia okay? Tell me you've got her."

"We have, Emma. She's safe and well. She's in the Lake District. Two officers are driving her home now. They won't be with you until the early hours of the morning, I hope that's okay?"

"It's fine. I just want her back."

"I hope you'll be throwing the book at the fiends who took her?" Mr Masterton shouted.

"It's all in hand. The team up north will be charging them, don't you worry about that, sir. It's all ended well, let's be grateful for that, eh?"

"Grateful? Are you insane, woman? If you hadn't gone round there and told them, this would never have happened. I'll be writing a letter of complaint to your superiors, you can be sure of that. Despicable behaviour on your part, absolutely disgusting."

"I'm sorry you feel that way, sir. I stand by my decision to tell them they had a grandchild. What I hadn't anticipated was them reacting the way they did. Grief can drive people to do things out of character."

"Yeah, well, so can rape, but you don't see us breaking the bloody law, do you?"

Before Sara could respond, he hung up on her. *I asked for that!*

She leaned back and rotated her head. Her neck was rigid with tension and cracked several times.

Carla knocked on the door and entered. "Everything all right? You look like you've just come out the other side of a tornado."

"I bloody feel like it. She's safe. I was just about to come and tell you all. I had to ring Emma to let her know first and had a run-in with her stepdad again. That man is trying my bloody patience to the limit."

"God, I'm so relieved the child is safe. We worked hard to ensure that happened."

"You're not wrong. Ask the girls if they're up for a quick drink after work—on me, of course."

"I can't make it, sorry. Gary wants to pop round his mum's this evening to discuss wedding plans with her."

"Lucky you. All right, we'll postpone it until we wrap the case up then. I'm going to check in with the other teams and then I think we should call it a day. I'll be out soon."

"Umm...going back to the investigation, I checked the archives because you mentioned the son was in court during the trial." She handed Sara a printed photo of the man. "He doesn't seem the type to want to take revenge."

"Is there a type nowadays? My gran used to say years ago about murderers having eyebrows that met in the middle. I used to laugh at her. But she insisted all the notorious murderers throughout history looked the same. I know it's hogwash, but you get what I mean. There's no telling what a murderer looks like these days."

"I hear you. Funny what runs through old folks' minds, eh? Anyway, what do you want to do about Teddy?"

"Nothing tonight. Let's get the child back home safely and then go round there tomorrow to have a word with him, yes? If he's involved, Tia's abduction might have had some bearing on his thinking, or is that me being guilty of wishful thinking? Either way, I'm exhausted, I know that."

"Yeah, you're not alone." Carla left the room.

Sara contacted Craig and Marissa. They were both on the move at the time, following each of the men under their surveillance home for the evening. She brought them up to date on what had happened with regard to Tia Wyatt and told them to remain with the men until seven and then call it a day.

Once she'd finished her call, she jotted down a few notes, mainly consisting of what they should do the following day to stay on top of things. She wanted to remain impartial where Teddy was concerned, didn't want to go barging in there, accusing him of all sorts without having any evidence to back up her claims. Her final call for the day was to Lorraine. "Hey, you. Are you free for a chat?"

"It depends whether you're going to tear me off a strip or not."

Sara's brow furrowed, and she clicked the end of her pen as she spoke. "Why would I do that?"

"Because I let you down."

"You have? Care to enlighten me?"

"I should have rung you about your brother."

"Oh, that! Yes, you should have, but I totally understand why you didn't."

"Phew! You do?"

"Yes, you were protecting me, or should I say my feelings. I appreciate that, Lorraine, no gripes from me, I promise."

"Sorry, love. The truth is, I didn't know how to tell you. I knew you'd be upset by the news and I struggled to justify my reasons for telling you. Then I got side-tracked with a couple more PMs, and before I knew it, Renshaw was ringing me, telling me that he'd broken the news to you and you were shell-shocked. I've been sitting here all afternoon…well, I've reached for the phone numerous times but chickened out of calling you."

"Don't be daft. Yes, you should have told me, but I understand why you didn't and don't blame you one iota, love. I certainly wouldn't fall out with you over this. My brother was his own worst enemy. I had no idea of the debt he was in. It came as a shock but, upon reflection, it didn't really. The drugs element blew my mind, though. I didn't put him down as a user."

"Whoa! Yes, there were marks on his arms. I'm waiting on the tox results to clarify if he was a regular user or not."

"But his throat was slit open, that's how he died, right?"

"Yep, I stand by that."

"Bloody hell. I have the daunting task of telling my parents now. I don't suppose we can keep the drugs element off the death certificate, can we? Bugger, ignore me, I didn't say that. Desperation rearing its ugly head, love."

"It's okay. I know you'd never ask me to alter my reports. It is what it is. Just be careful when you tell them."

"Yep, I'll do that. Do you have anything else for me, regarding the three murders?"

"Yes. Tox reports are back on all three victims, and Trazodone was used, presumably to sedate the men during their capture."

"Okay, is that a common drug? I can't say I've heard of it before."

"It's generally used as an anti-depressant and is thought to aid insomnia. It's commonly used in care homes for the elderly, I believe."

"Right. Well, at least that's something. I don't suppose you can tell if the men were sedated all the time or whether they were only initially knocked out to give the culprit the chance to abduct them?"

"I can't really tell, although saying that, I only found one pinprick in the neck of each victim when I examined them."

Sara fell silent. "Umm...fair enough. Anything else?"

"No, not really. Sorry."

"Don't be. You've been brilliant as usual. Enjoy your evening. Have you got any plans?"

"Nothing except to curl up in bed with a takeaway and a good book. I'm going through the Kathy Reichs series that was adapted for TV at the moment."

"Is that the *Bones* series?"

"That's the one. Pretty damn good factually, which makes a bloody change. What about you?"

"Nothing much. Mark and I will probably recap the wedding plans; only a few weeks to go now."

"You sound down in the dumps. Try not to let your brother's death spoil your wedding plans, love."

"I'll try hard not to, although, I've got to break the news to my parents yet."

"What? You haven't told them he's dead yet?"

"No, I mean, yes, I've told them that but not about the drugs or the loan shark element."

"My advice would be not to say anything for now. You shouldn't have been told the truth yet anyway. Just act dumb, get the wedding out the way, and then tell them afterwards if Luke hasn't."

"I'll take your advice on that one then. Thanks, Lorraine. Speak soon."

"Okay, I'm always here if you need to chat, you hear me?"

"You're a star. Ditto, and I mean that."

"I know you do. Now, go home and get some rest."

"On my way." She hung up and ran through the conversation again in her head as she made her way into the incident room. "What have you managed to find out about Teddy Masterton, guys? Specifically, what job he does, because something has come to light that may help us."

Christine looked down at her notebook. "He works in a care home. The Cedar Lodge care home out at Great Malvern."

"Interesting, so he travels to work every day?"

Christine nodded. "Either drives or possibly takes the train, who knows?"

"Carla and I will visit the family home tomorrow to see if he's there. If not, then we'll fly out to Great Malvern. It's been a while since I visited that area."

"Good time to go sightseeing," Carla mumbled.

"Wind your neck in, you cranky mare, I wasn't suggesting going on a picnic trip. Anyway, the tox reports are back. All three victims were knocked out by a sedative. My take is he's probably picked it up from the supply cupboard at the nursing home. Let's throw the towel in for the day, we could all do with the rest. Great work today, ladies."

The four of them left the station together. Sara called in at the supermarket to pick up a freshly made pizza and a bottle of wine, knowing that she had chips in the freezer at home. An easy slam-it-in-the-oven type of meal.

Mark walked through the front door around half an hour after she'd got home. He hugged her tightly. "Good day?"

"Not really, you?"

"Not really."

They laughed and kissed. It felt good to finally be in his arms.

"I cheated and bought pizza on the way home, don't hate me for it."

"As if I could ever hate you. You must have read my mind, it's just what my stomach was crying out for. Will it be long?" He opened the oven to have a look.

"Ten to fifteen minutes. Why, what did you have in mind?" She grinned and waggled her eyebrows.

"Sorry to disappoint you, a quick shower and a change of clothes."

Sara slapped his arm. "Go on, get out of my sight. There was me trying to be all romantic, and there's you, only concerned about getting freshened up."

"After the day I've had, I dread to think what lingering smells are lurking on my blasted clothes. I'll make it up to you later."

"Promises, promises. I bet you'll be fast asleep on the couch before ten."

He sped out of the room and ran up the stairs, shouting over his shoulder, "Probably. Why break the habit of a lifetime, eh?"

Sara poured them both a glass of wine and laid the table. One last check on the pizza and shake of the chips, and she could relax for the next five minutes. She chose that time to ring her sister.

"Hi, Lesley, how's it going?"

"I was going to ring you tonight, see if you'd heard anything."

Sara sighed. "I have. The trouble is, it's not good news, and I need to shield Mum and Dad. If they find out…well, I dread to think what will happen to their health. Can I trust you to keep your trap shut?"

"There's no need to be like that, of course you can trust me. What do you know?"

"I need you to be honest with me first."

"Always, what about?"

"Did you know Tim was in debt?"

"He mentioned it a while back. You know me, when he started talking about money, I tended to switch off. What are you getting at?"

She inhaled a large breath. "I have it on good authority from the inspector leading the case that he was up to his eyeballs in debt."

"Seriously? How much are we talking about here, Sara?"

"Over a hundred grand. He owed the money to a couple of loan sharks."

"Sodding hell. Oh heck, what are Mum and Dad going to say when they find out?"

"That's the dilemma facing us. My take is that we shouldn't tell them, there's no telling what it'll do to their health if we do."

"There is that. Shit, did he drink himself to death to escape the debts then?"

"Nope, Lesley, he was murdered. Whoever killed him slit his throat. Also, did you know he was a user?"

"No, I did not." Her sister cried.

"Are you okay? I knew I shouldn't have told you over the phone, love."

"I'm fine. It's such a shock. I feel so guilty about his death, for not keeping in touch with him over the last few months. He was bringing me down, though. I've had enough hassle of my own to deal with… well, you know that."

"Of course you have. Don't feel bad, hon. I get the guilt issue, it's running through like a fast-flowing river. It's all such a bloody mess. We need to make sure Mum and Dad don't find out, though for now. Agreed?"

"Totally. What about the death certificate, won't that have the facts on it?"

"Yes. I'll make sure it comes to me and I can deny having it, postpone it for a few weeks, maybe get the funeral and the wedding out of the way first, see what effect that has on their health and go from there. What do you think?"

"I think you have it all sussed out, thank God. Glad the decision hasn't fallen on my shoulders. I don't think I would have coped with it at all."

"Okay, that's settled then. I have to go, my dinner is ready now. Take care, sis."

"Wait, one last thing. What about his debts? Are the loan sharks likely to come after us for payment?"

"I bloody hope not, the thought never crossed my mind. I'll have a word with the SIO, see what he reckons, hopefully he'll arrest them soon. Promise me you won't lose sleep over it? I know what you're like and how things tend to fester."

"I promise. Let me know when you can. Thanks for ringing."

"I will. Speak soon. And Lesley…"

"Yes?"

"I don't say this often enough, I love you and I'm always here for you if ever you get into trouble."

"I know you are. I love you, too, and the same goes for you, okay? We're all we've got now."

"Apart from Mum and Dad."

She ended the call and put the phone on the worktop. Mark drifted into the room a few minutes later, smelling of musk aftershave or deodorant, she wasn't sure which, his hair damp from the shower.

"Ready for dinner?"

"Looking forward to it. Cheers." He sipped at his wine. "Did I hear you talking to someone?"

"Lesley. I broke the news about Tim."

"Am I missing something here?"

She thumped the side of her temple and cut the pizza. "Sorry, I rang earlier to tell you—you were too busy to take my call."

"I'll dish up the chips. What have you found out?"

"He was in debt to two loan sharks and he was murdered."

He tugged on her arm, forcing her to look at him. "Are you pulling my plonker?"

"I wish I was. Sorry to sound so blasé about it. To be honest with you, I was shocked at the time when Renshaw told me, but it's had time to sink in and, well, nothing surprises me where Tim was concerned. He was definitely the wrong 'un in the family. Saying that, I never expected him to go out like this."

"I'm so sorry, Sara. Will you tell your parents?"

"Not anytime soon. I don't think they could handle it, do you?"

"Very wise. Bugger, what a shocker. Will you arrest the loan sharks?"

"Renshaw will deal with it. He has both men under surveillance, been trying to bring them down for years, apparently. Let's hope he's successful. I've had enough shit like that to deal with over the years."

"Yeah, you're right. They're not likely to come after us, are they?" Panic sparked in his eyes.

"No fear of that. I'm doing everything I can to ensure that doesn't happen, love. Promise me you won't worry about it? I'd hate for anything to drive a wedge between us either before or after the wedding."

"Come here." He hugged her tightly and kissed the top of her head. "Nothing will ever come between us."

"Good. Let's eat, I'm starving."

## 12

"Good night last night?" Sara asked her partner on the drive out to the Mastertons' house the following morning.

"So-so. Gary had a tough physio session, and I took the brunt of his anger afterwards, nothing new there."

"Well, you need to sort that out, Carla, he has no right taking either his anger or frustration out on you."

"I know. I accept it for what it is. He doesn't mean to do it." Carla stared out of the window as if doing so would put an end to the conversation.

Sara sighed and took the hint. Carla deserved better than that. She'd seen Gary through some of his darkest days, and it was wrong of him to take his frustrations out on her when all she was trying to do was help him. She hated the thought of him putting on her and treating her like shit.

"I'm always here for you, you know that, right?"

"I do. Things are hunky-dory, Sara. Just concentrate on your own relationship and keep your nose out of mine."

*Whoa! Well, that told me, didn't it? I fear for you, my girl, you're not deceiving me at all.*

Sara didn't bother responding and instead put her foot down.

*Run For Your Life*

Carla's hands clung to the passenger seat. Sara had to suppress a chuckle. She could be so evil at times.

"Are you ready for this?" Sara pulled up outside the cottage.

"Yep. We're not going to be popular, are we?"

"I doubt it. We'll have each other for support."

"Yeah. I know. Sorry for snapping earlier. Got things going on in my head that I need to work through. It was nothing personal, I promise."

"You're fine. The offer still stands. I will say one thing, though, if you'll allow me to."

"Go for it."

"This should be the happiest of times for you, planning your wedding."

"Yep, I get that. That's what I need to figure out. We'll chat later, once I get my head around things, okay? I'm not shutting you out."

"All right." Sara squeezed Carla's knee. "Hang in there."

They left the car and walked up the path to the front door. Sara raised her hand to ring the bell only to find Mr Masterton had anticipated their arrival and had opened it already.

"Hello, Mr Masterton. All right if we come in for a quick chat?"

"Tia is home, if that's what this is about."

"It isn't, sir, although I'm glad to hear it. May we?"

He relented and gestured for them to enter the cottage.

Mrs Masterton stood in the hallway, drying her hands on a tea towel. "Hello there. I've just put the kettle on, would you like a drink?"

"That would be lovely, thank you. Two coffees, white with one sugar." Sara smiled and slipped past her into the lounge.

"All right, take a seat and tell me why you're here," Mr Masterton ordered, his tone stilted and unfriendly, the total opposite to how his wife had spoken to them.

"Is Emma here?"

"Where else would she be? Don't tell me you want proof?"

Sara grinned. "I'd like her to be here for this conversation, if it's all the same to you, sir."

"Good heavens, why? Don't you think that girl has been through enough over the years, more importantly, the last twenty-four hours?"

"Please, I don't want to cause any friction, sir."

He mumbled something as he left the room that sounded to Sara's ears like *then leave us alone!*

Emma returned with her father a few minutes later. Mrs Masterton also joined them with a tray of mugs which she handed out.

"You're very kind, thank you." Sara accepted the mug and held it in both hands. "How is Tia?"

Emma smiled. "She seems fine after her adventure, no damage done."

"That's good to hear. I'm glad she's back where she belongs."

"No thanks to you," Ben Masterton barked.

"They had a right to know. Maybe I'm at fault for telling them so soon after their son's murder. Which brings me back to the reason I'm here today. There appears to be a member of your family missing."

The Mastertons glanced at each other and then at Emma.

Mr Masterton acted as the spokesperson for the family as predicted. "Teddy, yes, he's absent."

"Absent? Can you tell me where he is?"

"Not really, no. He's taken a few days off."

"From work?" Sara probed, her intrigue piqued.

"From work, from us. He's gone away. All of this has been too much for him," Mr Masterton confirmed.

"All of what? When did he leave, sir?"

"I don't know. A few days ago."

"It was Thursday," Emma confirmed.

"Thank you. Now, perhaps you'll tell us where he's gone?"

"We can't. He just took off, didn't even tell us he was going. He even took the dog with him," Mrs Masterton said.

"Dog? You have a dog? What breed of dog?"

"Yes, Tyson. He's a Rottweiler," Emma said. "I was worried about him, you know, what with Tia being around. He's a big softie, best dog we've ever had. Very protective of the family."

"I see. Where do you think he's likely to have gone, with the dog in tow? I should imagine his options are limited."

The three family members remained silent and shook their heads.

"Please, this is important," Sara urged. She took a sip of her hot drink and watched their reactions closely.

"We can't think of anywhere. Why? What does his absence have to do with anything?"

"How long has he worked at the care home?" Sara asked, ignoring Mr Masterton's question.

"Five years or more. He loves it there, looking after the old folk," Mrs Masterton replied, a proud smile lighting up her subtly wrinkled face.

"That's wonderful to hear. Has he ever been in bother with his employers?"

"No. I repeat, what's this about?" Mr Masterton demanded. He rose to his feet and stood over by the inglenook fireplace.

"Can you try calling him for me? I take it he has a mobile phone?"

Mr Masterton tutted and grabbed his phone off the table. He scrolled through and punched at a number. He shook his head and put the phone on speaker.

Sara listened to the dead tone filling the room. "Does he often turn his phone off?"

"No, it's very unlike him," Mr Masterton admitted.

"Can you give me his number? I'll see if I can get a trace on it, make sure he's okay."

He handed the phone to Carla to jot down the number. She nipped into the hallway to ring the station and came back into the room shaking her head. "Nope, no trace. Maybe he removed the SIM card."

Sara sighed. "What do you know of your son's whereabouts over the past week?"

Mrs Masterton spoke out first. "As far as we knew he was going to work as normal. He came home on Wednesday telling us he'd been given unexpected time off and he was going away. He left the room to get packed, and that was the last we saw of him, well...the next morning."

"I see. And you didn't think to question him?"

"Our son is a grown man, we don't keep him under lock and key and demand to know the ins and outs of what he's up to," Mr Masterton stated harshly.

"Fair enough. Please, I need you to try and think of where he might be. Do you have a holiday home somewhere perhaps?"

"No. We're not made of money. We can't think of anywhere. Why do you need to speak with him?"

"We'd like to speak to him regarding the investigation, that's all." Sara skirted around the issue of him possibly being the murderer just in case the family were lying and did know where he was hiding out.

"We'll let him know when we see him. Everyone is entitled to time away, that's not a crime, is it?" Mr Masterton smiled tautly.

"No, it's not a crime, but the timing is questionable to say the least."

"He's a sensitive lad. He went through a lot during his sister's court case."

"In what respect?" Sara asked.

"He was upset. First that Emma got attacked and, secondly, that the five men got off."

"Understandable him being cut up about that, I suppose. Okay, we'd better get on the road again. You've got my number. If he should get in touch, will you please ring me?"

"Of course we will. I'll show you out." Mr Masterton crossed the room to the door.

His wife and daughter appeared quiet, and Sara couldn't help but wonder if they weren't hiding something. In the end, she brushed the feeling aside and joined Carla at the front door with Mr Masterton.

"We'll be in touch if we have any further questions, sir. I'm glad your granddaughter arrived home safely."

"Believe me, so am I. There would have been hell to pay if she hadn't. I'm still going to write to your superiors about all of this."

"That's your prerogative. Enjoy the rest of your day."

On the journey back to the station, Carla asked, "What now? You think they're covering for the son?"

Sara clenched and unclenched her hands around the steering wheel as she thought. "Something didn't feel right back there. Whether they were covering for him or not, that remains to be seen. Oh, I don't know, maybe I'm reading too much into this and they were reacting like any normal family would after a child had been abducted."

"Maybe. It's not getting any easier, is it?"

"You can say that again."

Sara mulled over what their next course of action should be. "We need to find his car. Run the plate through the ANPR cameras, see if we can track his movements and discover where he's hiding out. I have an inkling he's not far and is going to strike again soon."

"Where does that leave us? With the surveillance angle?"

"We'll do our best to keep the two men under surveillance for the next week. After that, they'll be on their own again. We're going to have to do a few stints ourselves, if you're up for that, just so the teams don't get bored."

"Yep, I'll do whatever we need to do to catch this bastard. Pretty worrying that he's using his dog, don't you think?"

"Yeah, that part really sticks in my throat because he's effectively signed the dog's death certificate—if he's the guilty party, that is."

"I don't think there's any doubt in my mind now, especially when the dog was mentioned."

"We still need to take a trip out to the nursing home. Maybe they'll be able to fill us in on his character et cetera."

"Maybe he's hiding out around there."

"You never know." Sara put her foot down and drove the forty-five minutes out to Great Malvern. The area tugged at her heart like it always did. The dramatic landscape and the fact she could see for hundreds of miles over several counties as they reached the summit sent a thrill chasing down her spine. "I love this place. I need to come here more often, it does something inexplicable to my soul."

She glanced briefly at Carla who was regarding her warily. "If you say so. It's a couple of large hills with a severe drop to me."

"Where's your zest for life gone, girl? Your sense of adventure?"

"Up the swanny for all I know. This place is just another tourist attraction that gets overwhelmed in the summer with hikers, much to the locals' disgust, I should imagine."

"I suppose so. Right, we're here. Let's see what they have to say about Master Masterton."

Carla rolled her eyes. "Did you have to prove me right? I had a feeling you'd spout that before very long."

Sara chuckled. "Delighted I haven't let you down then, mardy arse."

"And you can keep my arse out of the conversation, if you don't mind."

They both laughed and left the car.

Sara produced her ID and showed it to the woman with pretty blue eyes sitting in the reception area. "Is it possible to speak to the person in charge? It's important."

"I'll get Mrs Finch for you. Do you want to take a seat while I try and locate her? I know she's on her rounds at the moment."

"Sure."

They took a seat, and Sara flicked through an interiors magazine which caught her eye on the table. "I'd love a conservatory or an orangery one day, wouldn't you?" She flashed Carla the picture that jumped out at her halfway through the magazine.

"Not really. All I see is extra housework. I hate cleaning windows as it is. To have one of those would be my worst bloody nightmare."

With that, a woman in her early thirties rushed towards them. "Hello there, I'm Charlotte Finch, how can I help you?"

Sara and Carla stood, and Sara introduced them. "If you're not too busy, we'd like a brief chat about a member of your staff."

"I can get back to my rounds later. Why don't we go into my office? This way."

They followed her behind the reception desk and up a small hallway to a larger-than-average office which overlooked a colourful courtyard. Sara was impressed by the outlook.

"Take a seat. Which member of staff are you here about?"

"Teddy Masterton." Sara watched for any type of reaction to the name. There was none.

"Ah, I see. He's on holiday at present, so you won't be able to see him, I'm afraid."

"That's okay. Did he mention where he was going?"

Mrs Finch appeared to contemplate the question for a while and then shook her head. "No, he didn't. Things have been pretty full-on around here for a few months, and a number of the staff have struggled with the changes we've been forced to make recently. I told a couple of them to take a break sooner than they needed to. Teddy jumped at the chance to take time off, however, he never said what his intentions were."

"I have to ask what his duties are, Mrs Finch."

"He's one of the juniors here. I know that sounds strange for his age, but he insisted he didn't want too much responsibility on his shoulders. He's so good with the patients, he loves them as much as they love him."

"That's nice to hear. So he's never been in any bother?"

Mrs Finch frowned and shook her head. "No. Why? What are you getting at? Why are you here asking these questions? Is Teddy in trouble with the police?"

"Not really. Cards on the table, we're investigating three serious crimes where sedatives have been involved."

Mrs Finch gasped and covered her mouth then instantly dropped her hand. "What's the name of the sedative?"

"Trazodone."

"Oh heck!"

"What's wrong, Mrs Finch?"

"We've had several vials of that go missing over the past year or so. Nothing recently. The last batch went missing around six months ago, if I remember rightly."

"What did you do about it?"

"We questioned all the staff. Everyone denied either stealing or breaking any of the bottles. It was a mystery, an unsolved one at that."

"Did Teddy have access to the medicines?"

"Yes. Bloody hell, are you telling me he's used it to cause harm to someone?"

"Possibly. At present, it's pure speculation."

"Oh my goodness. Well, that's one person I never had down for stealing it."

Sara tilted her head. "May I ask why?"

"He's such an amiable type of chap, I never have any hassle with him. He's always putting the residents first. Constantly works overtime if he's in the middle of doing something important for one of the residents. He's an amazing, caring individual."

"That's some character assessment. Are you sure he didn't mention where he was spending this week?"

"No, I'm certain. Have you asked his family?"

"Yes, they don't know either."

"Would you mind telling me what type of investigation he's connected with?"

"Three murders. As I've already stated, it's a tenuous link right now. You can understand our need to contact him ASAP."

"Yes, of course I can. I'm sorry, I wish I could be of more help to you. I'll be devastated to learn he's behind what you're suggesting. Have you met him?"

"No, we haven't had the pleasure as yet. I know it's a long shot, but is there anywhere in the grounds where he could possibly be hiding out?"

"No. We have the main house and the garden. There's a small garden shed where the groundsman keeps his equipment, but it's tiny, I couldn't see Teddy staying there. I'm sure I would've heard about it by now if he was in there."

"Well, okay, thanks very much for speaking to us." Sara had a sudden idea. "I don't suppose you have a contact number for him, just in case he's given you a different number to the one his parents use to make contact with him?"

"Let me get his file, hold on a second." She retrieved a file from the cabinet and wheeled her chair back under the desk. "Here we go." She read out the number, and Carla jotted it down.

Sara compared it to the one she'd rung earlier and shook her head.

"Nope, it's the same number. It was worth a try." Disappointed, she and Carla left Cedar Lodge nursing home and drove back to the station.

As soon as they entered the incident room, they got down to the business of trying to find Teddy's car on the ANPR system. Sara had a feeling this task was going to keep her, and her limited team, busy for the next few days.

## 13

Sara's frustrations had mounted to a crescendo over the past four days. They were now into Wednesday of the following week and still no further forward. The only saving grace was that the surveillance she'd put in place had appeared to have done the trick of keeping the final two men safe. However, they were into their seventh day on that, and at seven o'clock, that indulgence was about to draw to a close.

Fed up with sitting in the station all day going nowhere, both physically and metaphorically speaking, Sara had decided she and Carla should be part of the final surveillance shifts. They split up. Sara went with Craig, and Carla drew the short straw and was assigned to work alongside Barry.

Sara and Craig sat outside B&Q all day, while Carla and Barry were stuck in the factory car park, babysitting 'Boy Wonder', otherwise known as Brad Iverson, who had apparently clocked the other members of the surveillance team watching him once or twice and had threatened them several times to back off and leave him alone. The team had shrugged off his offensive language and stuck to him like sticky willy weed.

At six o'clock, Sara was in the process of following Aaron back to his mother's house. She decided to check on the others to see how they were doing. "How's it hanging?"

Carla answered the phone. "Fine, we're just leaving now. He's clocked we're with him and glared at us but said nothing so far. The more I see of this shit the more I despise him. You did say he was the leader of the gang, back in the day, didn't you?"

"Correct. You can tell he's living up to his 'I'm the boss' reputation, right?"

"Yep. We'll stick with him another hour then call it a day."

"I was about to suggest the same. See you back at the station."

Sara ended the call. "One more hour and then we get our lives back."

"Where does that leave us, though, boss? What with Teddy Masterton still AWOL?"

Sara hitched up a shoulder. "Your guess is as good as mine, Craig. We'll put our heads together in the morning. It'll be good to be finally back to full strength."

"I bet. Can't say I've enjoyed babysitting these guys. Boring doesn't bloody touch it."

"Sorry, it's a necessary part of the job on occasions. The glamour of being a serving police officer, eh?"

They both laughed.

∞

"I can't wait to get out of here at seven," Carla stated, settling into her seat once she'd parked up outside Brad's home.

"I bet he'll be relieved to see the back of us as well. Ay up! What's this?" Barry pointed at the sleek sports car which had haphazardly parked a few spaces in front of them.

Carla's gaze flicked between the car and Brad's house. He opened the door and stood on the doorstep beaming at the woman as she got out of the car. She trotted up to him in ridiculously high heels and kissed him on the lips. He ushered her inside and checked no one else saw the girl enter.

"That wasn't his girlfriend, I take it?"

"Nope, she's a brunette, not a ditsy blonde. Shit, he's heading our way for another confrontation. I'll handle him."

"Be careful," Carla said.

Barry kicked open his door as Brad approached. "What the fuck are you guys still hanging around me for?"

"You need to calm down, mate," Barry told him with a raised hand.

Iverson fisted Barry in the face. "I'm not your *mate*. Now fucking back off."

Carla shot out of the car. "Barry, are you okay?"

Barry lunged at Iverson. "I'll have you for assaulting a police officer, you cretin."

"Bring it on, mate. Go on, fuck off and take this bitch with you. I've had it with you guys." He went to walk away.

Before Carla could stop him, Barry bounced onto his feet and thumped Iverson in the back of the neck.

Iverson was livid. His face gnarled with anger, he marched towards Carla and Barry. Carla stood in front of her colleague.

"Come on, make my day. Hit me, you bastard. After all, you take pleasure in hurting women, don't you?" Carla goaded.

He threw Carla out of the way. He was far stronger than he looked and a lucky punch knocked Barry unconscious. Then he returned to Carla and hovered over her.

Iverson turned around at the squeal of tyres. A metal bar struck him on the side of the head.

"What the fuck are you doing?" Carla asked the man dressed in black. She scrambled to her feet.

"Get on with your life. This fucker doesn't need police protection any more."

Carla grappled with the pepper spray attached to her belt, but the man struck out, and she took a blow to her temple. Everything went black.

. . .

Carla woke up a while later to check on Barry. He was still out cold, blood oozing from the back of his head, covering the pavement. Her neck and head felt leaden, and it was difficult to keep them held up. The woman who had got out of the sports car was screaming by the front door, and a crowd had gathered.

A man rushed over to help Carla. "Are you all right?"

"Did you see what happened?" Carla asked him.

"No, I just pulled up. I'll ring an ambulance. Stay there, don't move, you've probably got concussion."

"I'm a police officer. I need to get my phone, I think it's in the car."

"I'll get that after I've placed the call."

She drifted off but could hear him urgently requesting an ambulance.

"Please, my phone. I need to call it in," Carla urged.

The man raced around the front of the car and fetched her phone.

Carla's vision was blurred. "Shit, I can't see the numbers. I need to contact the station. Shit, shit, shit!"

"Please, don't worry. Take your time to come round."

"I don't have the time. Shit. Press number three for me."

The man did as instructed, then he placed the phone to her ear. "Sara, it's me. He's gone."

"What? Carla, are you all right?"

"We both got attacked. Barry's in a bad way."

"How? What happened?"

"I can't tell you. A man, probably Masterson, showed up." Carla realised she'd got his name wrong, but she knew Sara would understand.

"All right. Stay there. I'm coming to get you."

"No. What about the other one, Aaron? Is he safe?"

"Yes, we're on our way back to the station. We'll make a detour and come and get you."

"No. Go back to Aaron. Please, don't come here."

"Okay. Keep in touch. Take care."

Sara blew out a breath, trying to relieve the panic burning her chest. "Shitting hell. I hope we're not too late."

Craig flicked on the siren, and the car fell silent except for the wailing noise surrounding them. Sara screeched to a halt outside Aaron's address. They'd seen the man safely home an hour before and remained there until seven. She threw open the car door and ran towards the house. She pounded on the door. It was opened by a woman in her late fifties.

"Is Aaron here?"

"No. A friend called to take him out for a drink."

"Where have they gone?"

She seemed puzzled by the question. "I don't know. Who are you?"

Sara grappled for and flashed her ID. "Police. I don't have time for this. Where did they go?"

"I don't know. Probably down The Swan, knowing Aaron."

"Which direction?"

"Left and right at the end of the road. What's going on?"

"Did they go by car?"

"The man had a van."

"Thanks, what colour?"

"Dark, either black or navy blue, I couldn't tell."

"Okay. Please, go back inside."

"Not until you tell me what's going on."

"Aaron could be in danger," Sara called over her shoulder, darting back to the car.

"You can't say that and leave me here wondering what the hell's happening to my son," the woman shouted after her.

Sara ignored her and jumped in the car. She rang the station and spoke to the desk sergeant. "Jeff, thank God you're still there. We've got an urgent situation on our hands, and I could do with uniforms' full cooperation."

"I was just clocking off...sod that, tell me what you need."

"Bless you." She ran through the details of what had occurred. He was as appalled as she was and promised to rally the troops. "We need to find that van, and quickly." An idea jumped into her whirling mind. "Do me a favour, I'm going to call Emma Wyatt. Can you get a car out to the Mastertons' cottage? I have an inkling she knows where her stepbrother is. We'll see if she goes after him despite rarely leaving the house. Use an unmarked car, if at all possible."

"I'm with you, good thinking. I'll get my best lads on it. They won't let you down."

"Fabulous. I'll give you five minutes to organise things—no, make it ten. Let me know when they're in place, and I'll make the call."

"You've got it."

Sara jumped in the car and drove to Iverson's house to see how Carla and Barry were. The ambulance had been and gone. Carla had refused to go and had called Gary to fetch her instead. He'd just arrived when they got there.

Sara shot out of the car and hugged Carla. "Shit! Look at the state of you. Why didn't you go to hospital?"

Gary tutted. "That's what I told her."

"Behave. I'm fine. My head's a little fuzzy but it's Barry I'm concerned about. He hadn't come around by the time the ambulance turned up."

"Poor guy. Look, I've got everything organised. I have a good feeling about this. Gary, take her home and tuck her up in bed for the night. Keep her away from the TV, okay?"

"Yep, I'll make sure that happens. Good luck. Come on, love, I'll pick up your car tomorrow."

"Thanks, guys. Sorry to have let you down, Sara. There was nothing I could do."

"Don't be silly. You haven't let me down, you did your best."

Sara's phone rang. She glanced at her watch. Eight minutes had passed since she'd called Jeff.

"Hey, I was getting ready to ring you. How's it going?"

"My two best men, Ackers and Watkins, are en route. They should be there in five minutes or so, if you can hold off making the call until then, boss."

"I can. I appreciate it, Jeff. Ring me when they get there, will you?"

"Sure."

She ended the call and watched Gary help Carla into the passenger seat of his car. She smiled and waved them off. Then she faced Craig and high-fived him. "We've got this. Are you up for a scrap tonight?"

"I'm all yours…er, you know what I mean, boss."

"I do." She held up her engagement ring. "I'm spoken for, remember."

His cheeks turned a fetching burgundy shade, and she laughed.

"I'm pulling your leg."

Jeff rang back, giving her the go-ahead to make the call.

Sara steadied her racing heart and then took the plunge. She raised her crossed fingers and rolled her eyes at Craig. "Wish me luck."

"Luck."

She dialled Emma's number. "Hi, Emma. This is DI Sara Ramsey, can you talk?"

Sara heard a door creak and then close. "Yes, I'm in the hallway. What can I do for you?"

"Emma, I'm begging you to tell me if you know where Teddy is."

There was a moment's hesitation before the young woman responded. "I don't know, I told you."

"Emma, this is really important. We know he's behind the murders, please help us. The thing is, he's abducted the final two men. I know they were out of order assaulting you the way they did, but please, don't let Teddy seek further retribution by killing the rest of the gang members."

"Shit! Don't do this to me. Don't put me in this situation. They deserve to die after what they did."

"So you do know where he is. Where's he keeping them, Emma? If you don't tell me, I'll come over there and arrest you for withholding evidence."

"That's bollocks. I know nothing. You can't prove anything."

"I'll find a way of pinning this on both of you, unless you're willing to help me."

"I know nothing."

The line went dead.

"Fuck. I've screwed it up."

"No, you haven't. Let's wait and see. If your hunch is right, she should make her move soon."

Sara paced the pavement, stopping dead when her phone jangled. "Hello?"

"It's Jeff. Ackers just called. She's on the move."

"Jesus, thank fuck for that. Sorry, Jeff, I thought I'd messed up for a moment there. Can you give the guys my number? I want direct contact with them. We'll meet up with them. Bloody hell, stand by, we could be in for a long night, love."

"I'll stick around, ensure things run smoothly at this end."

"You're a saint, I don't care what your wife says about you."

"Cheeky. Go get him, or them, we're right behind you."

"Cheers, Jeff."

She ended the call and got back in the car. Ackers contacted her and left the line open a few minutes later. Sara gestured for Craig to swap seats and handed him the keys to her car. "Be gentle with her."

"I will," he promised, revving the engine like a boy racer would on a brand-new circuit he was about to be let loose on.

"What have I done?" She groaned.

Craig took off in the direction of the city. He listened to Ackers' instructions and took the appropriate actions. Before long, they were sitting on Ackers' tail.

"Let's give her a bit of room, boys, hold back a little. I reckon she's savvier than she's letting on. She conned me into thinking she was the innocent victim in all of this. Maybe she was once upon a time, not now, though."

They followed the car across town out into the sticks to Melrose Forest. She drove down a narrow track. "Hold back, let her go. We'll give her a few minutes and then head in there after her."

Sara's patience was tauter than a newly fastened guitar string. "All right. Ackers, wait there. We'll jump in your car."

Craig parked up in a nearby lay-by, and they ran back to join the other two men. After a quick introduction, Watkins drove down the bumpy track. The light was fading, mostly due to the dense canopy of trees overhead. Sara got her phone out and prepared to use the torch if necessary.

"What's that?" Craig pointed ahead.

The other three squinted.

"Some sort of shack, a cabin. This has to be it," Sara replied. "But where's her car?"

"It's probably around the rear. Hang on, I see something glinting. Yes, it's a car bumper— no, there are two vehicles. One's a van," Ackers said.

"He's here. Right, I'm going to call for backup before we go any further." She contacted Jeff, and he agreed to send reinforcements to join them ASAP. "That's our backs covered. Can you stop the car here, and we'll go the rest of the way on foot?"

The four of them left the vehicle and used the tree trunks to shield their progress towards the cabin. There was one small window at the front with a light glowing as if guiding their way.

"Let's be cautious. No sudden moves. We'll monitor the situation first, got that?"

The three men agreed and took up their positions again. Together they inched their way closer. Raised voices came from inside the cabin. A gun went off, sending shock waves between the officers.

"Fuck. Well, we knew he was going to be armed. Ackers, have you got a Taser back in the car?"

"Nope, I've got it in my pocket, ma'am. I used to be in the boy scouts and always come prepared."

"Fan-bloody-tastic. You'd better go ahead of us then."

He inched past her, and they crept forward, making sure none of them stepped on a twig that would alert the people inside. More shouting sounded. Sara's heart pounded harder until it affected her breathing.

There was a window on the side of the cabin. Sara asked Ackers, who was the tallest, to peer through it. He peeked in and pulled back quickly. He held up four fingers. "Three men and one girl, plus a mean-looking Rotti."

"That's Teddy, Emma and the two men they've abducted." In the distance, sirens wailed. "Bloody hell, nothing like announcing you're on your way."

Ackers peered through the window again. "I don't think they've noticed. The two men are tied up. One of them is writhing in agony, looks like he's been shot in the knee."

"Okay, well, we're going to have to be careful, we don't want any more injuries, or worse still, fatalities."

"How do you want to approach this?" Ackers asked.

"You're going to have to go in first, are you up for that?"

"Of course. I'll take out the bloke with the gun."

"We'll be right behind you."

A growling noise sounded on the other side of the wall.

"Shit! The dog has probably heard us," Sara suggested.

"We need to take him out of the equation first. Wait, the bloke holding the gun is shouting at the men. Wait, he's untying them," Ackers replied.

"That's Teddy Masterton. What the heck is he up to? Keep watching, Ackers."

Ackers gave them a running commentary. "Jesus, he's handed each of them a knife. The skinny one is quivering like a bloody blancmange. Fuck, he's told them to fight to the death. The loser will get hunted down and ripped to shreds by Tyson."

Sara sighed and shook her head. "Barbaric. Which is the worst fate?"

"You tell me," Ackers replied.

The dog continued to growl.

"It's no good, we've got to try and make a move."

Craig glanced over his shoulder. Dozens of officers were coming towards them. He motioned for them to take cover behind the trees.

"Are you ready?" Sara asked Ackers, the only officer who was armed.

"I'll give it my best shot. Can you guys deal with the dog?"

Craig picked up a nearby club-shaped bit of branch and nodded. "Leave him to me."

Sara raised her thumb. Ackers eased open the back door and entered the cabin. Sara shoved Craig ahead of her and brought up the rear with Watkins.

All hell let loose as soon as they entered the back door. The dog clamped his mouth around Ackers' arm. He cried out and thumped the animal in the head, then Craig bashed it with the club. The dog ran off, out of the cabin and into the forest.

"Teddy, give yourself up?" Sara shouted.

It was a Mexican standoff. He was holding a gun at them, and Ackers had the Taser pointed at Teddy's chest.

"Let Teddy do this, please?" Emma pleaded from the other side of the room.

"No, Emma. Stand back, we won't let Teddy win, not this time. Teddy, put your gun down. We have armed police outside, surrounding this place." It was a white lie but a necessary one.

"As if. Drop your weapon." Teddy glared at Ackers.

"You drop yours," Ackers shouted.

Emma moved to stand between them, putting herself in harm's way. "Stop it! Teddy hasn't done anything wrong. These bastards have ruined my life, they need to pay for what they did." Tears dripped onto her cheeks.

Sara took a step closer. "Emma, this is wrong, surely you can see that?"

"It's not. You lot let them off. All Teddy is doing is righting that wrong. You think it's okay for men to swan around, raping women when it suits them?" She prodded her temple with her finger. "Teddy understands the damage their crime has done to my head over the years. The nightmares I've suffered. The torture I've had to endure seeing Tia grow up, a constant reminder of the barbaric…" Her voice caught in her throat at the mention of her child's name.

"I know, love. It couldn't have been easy for you, I realise that, but truly, this isn't the way to try and compensate. Please, Teddy, let them go. Let us deal with them the correct way. Several parents of the other victims have already admitted the boys lied. Let's gather the evidence and retry them. That's the answer, *not* this."

"They deserve to die for what they did to Emma. The court and your lot called her a liar. You're all responsible for the distress she's suffered over the years. You haven't been there to see her, doubting her place in this world. Only a few months ago…she tried to end it."

Emma turned to face him. "But I didn't. You got me through it, Teddy, only you."

"Because I love you, Emma, I always have." His voice lowered to a whisper for a moment, and then he glared at the two men in front of him and drove the butt of the gun into each of their midriffs. "You don't deserve to live, you bastards."

"Do it." Sara urged Ackers to take the shot.

The Taser struck Teddy in the chest. He sank to his knees and cried out, violently shaking as the fifty thousand volts surged through his body.

"Shut it off," Sara ordered. She rushed to grab Emma who was about to crouch and tend to her stepbrother. "Come on, let's get you out of here."

"No, I want to make sure he's okay. Please, help him."

"He'll be fine. Craig, take her outside."

Craig stepped forward and grasped Emma's arm.

Ackers and Watkins checked Teddy over and then pulled him to his feet and escorted him out of the cabin. He tried to wriggle free, but they held firm.

"You two," Sara snarled at Brad and Aaron. "Get out of my frigging sight. Brad, you'll be seen by a doctor and then charged for assaulting two of my officers. Aaron, I'll send a uniformed officer around to see you in a few days to take a statement."

"Hey, you can't speak to us like that," Brad snarled.

"Can't I? How else should I speak to rapists, eh?" She poked Brad in the chest a few times. "I meant what I said. I'm going to get the CPS to reopen Emma's case against you. Don't go thinking you've got away with this a second time, boys."

Brad glared at her. "Yeah, bring it on, bitch. Our barristers will get us off again."

Sara's lip curled. "You're scum. Don't forget I have witness statements from the other gang members' families to back up Emma's claims this time around, plus I'll volunteer to speak on her behalf as well. I guarantee you'll go down for this…better late than never, eh?"

Sara watched a couple of officers take the men away and let out a relieved sigh. "Shit! What a frigging day and a half that was."

And it wasn't over yet. There were still the interviews with Emma and Teddy to attend once she got back to the station.

Thankfully, the interviews went smoother than Sara had predicted. Teddy had admitted to all the murders and had gone over every detail in his plan. His account was callous, showing little or no remorse. The only regret he had was that Sara had prevented him from killing the final two men.

Emma had sworn that she had nothing to do with the murders. The only reason she was at the cabin was because Teddy had taken her there months before, showing off his latest acquisition. Sara was willing to forgive her for not revealing where the cabin was in the circumstances. Neither of his parents had known about the cabin, so Sara had reprimanded herself for doing Mr Masterton an injustice, thinking that he was guilty of covering for Teddy.

Sara drove Emma home herself. She dropped her off with the promise that she would keep her word and help her to obtain the justice she was after against Aaron Thornton and Brad Iverson, despite what Iverson had said.

She drove home, mentally and physically exhausted. She rang Carla on the way and assured her that Teddy was behind bars at last. Then she rang the hospital to check how Barry was. The nurse told her that he'd just regained consciousness and was being a pain in the arse, refusing to stay in hospital. Sara had issued a warning, via the nurse, for him to remain there overnight and to reassess his condition in the morning.

# EPILOGUE

Sara was filled with mixed emotions over the next week. With the case now wrapped up there was the paperwork to deal with and CPS to contact regarding Emma's original rape case. They agreed to look into it in detail for her.

On Friday of that week, she took the day off to attend her brother's funeral. He was laid to rest at the local church in Marden. Her mother was still shrouded in guilt. Sara still hadn't divulged the true nature of his death yet, agreeing with the undertaker to present the death certificate to her so her parents didn't see it. She had decided to reveal all after her wedding the following day.

The wake was an intimate affair, only family and a few of the neighbours attended. Sara and Mark made their excuses to leave early and set off on the long drive up to Scotland.

The wedding took place in the grand surroundings of Castle Drogon at three on Saturday. Sara anxiously got ready an hour before the service, her thoughts with her family and whether they would make it on time for the ceremony.

Her anxiety was uncalled for as she spotted her father's car arrive with fifty minutes to spare.

"Sara, you look beautiful," her mother cried the moment she stepped into the room.

Even Lesley and her father had the odd tear in their eyes.

"Aye, she does that." Her father squeezed her tightly and kissed her on the cheek.

"I'm so glad you could all make it. I know it's been a bugger of a week for all of us."

"Hush now. Let's not think about that. Tim's gone, let's concentrate on the here and now and make this day as special as your first wedding."

Sara laughed. "Thanks, Mum." Her smile dropped. "I hope this one lasts longer than the first."

"It will," Lesley assured her. "Come on, Mum, we should get going, take our seats downstairs."

They both hugged Sara and wished her luck then left the room.

Her father took her hand. "Not having any doubts are you, love?"

"No, Dad. A silly thought just crossed my mind, that's all."

"What was that?"

"I wondered if Philip would approve of me getting married again."

"I'm sure he'd be up there, cheering you both on, sweetheart. What's there to dislike about Mark? He's the most genuine man I think I've ever had the pleasure of meeting, with the exception of Philip, of course."

"Thanks, Dad, that means a lot." Sara kissed her father's cheek, and at the same time a million butterflies took flight in her stomach.

"It's the truth. Be happy, my darling."

Sara held up her crossed fingers. "Okay, let's get this over with."

They descended the sweeping stone staircase under the gazes of the attendees. Sara concentrated on her steps, not wishing to tumble down and make a fool of herself. Once she was safely at the bottom, she glanced around the guests and smiled, delighted that all her team were in attendance with their respective partners. She proceeded down the aisle and spotted Lorraine and Carla sitting next to each other near the front. She frowned and mouthed, "Where's Gary?" to Carla.

Carla shook her head and mouthed back, "I'll fill you in later. Good luck."

Sara was confused. Why was she here alone?

Carla motioned for her not to dwell on things and to move on. She did just that and joined Mark at the front of the majestic hall where the celebrant was waiting to do his part.

Mark leaned over and whispered, "You'll always have my heart, Sara. I love you."

She smiled, her cheeks warming under his close scrutiny. "I love you, too. It's not too late for you to back out, you know."

He chuckled. "As if that's ever been an option."

## THE END

Dear Reader,

What a dilemma Sara had solving this case. But as usual, Sara and her team came to the rescue in her own inimitable way. An intriguing tale nevertheless, I'm sure you'll agree.

Have you read the bestselling, award-winning Justice series yet? Here's the link to the first book in this gripping, fast-paced thriller series CRUEL JUSTICE

Thank you for your support as always. If you could find it in your heart to leave a review, I'd be eternally grateful, they're like nectar from the Gods to authors.

Happy reading
M A Comley

# KEEP IN TOUCH WITH M A COMLEY

Newsletter
http://smarturl.it/8jtcvv

BookBub
www.bookbub.com/authors/m-a-comley

Blog
http://melcomley.blogspot.com

Join my special Facebook group to take part in monthly giveaways.

Readers' Group